Crescent
Moon

Crescent Moon

Alden R. Carter

Holiday House / New York

Acknowledgments

Many thanks to all who helped with *Crescent Moon*, particularly my mother, Hilda Carter Fletcher; my editor, Regina Griffin; my children, Brian and Siri; and my friends Don Beyer, Dean Markwardt, Steve Sanders, Larry Lynch, Dave Samter, Bill Reiss, and Jeff and Duffy Gaier. As always, my wife, Carol, deserves much of the credit.

Library of Congress Cataloging-in-Publication Data
Carter, Alden R.
Crescent Moon / by Alden R. Carter. — 1st ed.
p.   cm.
Summary: Living in the logging area of northern Wisconsin
during the early 1900s, thirteen-year-old Jeremy helps his uncle
carve a statue of a Chippewa maiden as a tribute
to the vanishing culture of her people.
ISBN 0-8234-1521-X
[1. Wood carving Fiction.   2. Uncles Fiction.   3. Ojibwa Indians
Fiction.   4. Indians of North America—Wisconsin Fiction.
5. Wisconsin Fiction.]   I. Title.
[PZ7.C2426Cr   1999b]
[Fic]—dc21   99-24654
CIP

For some friends:
Larry Lynch, Tim Hirsch,
and Steve and Kathy Sanders

Chapter I

☽

Jeremy heard the roar not long after first light. It wasn't so much a roar as the promise of a roar, so faint that he doubted for a moment whether he'd heard it at all. But when he lifted the window to let in the May morning, and with it all the sounds and smells of river and town, he clearly heard the growl of the river. And though the breeze was cool, it was anticipation that prickled the hair on the back of his neck and made the goose bumps rise on his arms. Because the growl would become a roar—a roar to shake the houses, the stores, and the very bricks of the streets of Eau Claire; a roar to shake the heart of every boy who'd ever dreamed of dancing on the river of logs that had come down the mighty Chippewa every spring for half a century, but after today would come no more.

Uncle Mac ran his palm across the neck of the carved horse's head. "It must be smoother. Especially here, behind the ears." The old man went back to his own workbench, where he was painting a wooden bear's head.

Jeremy sighed and started sanding behind the horse's ears. "We ought to get a machine to do this."

Uncle Mac dipped a brush and began giving the bear's teeth another coat of white paint. "Machines have no love in them. They can't do work like a man can with his hands, his eyes, and a few tools."

Another day Jeremy might have argued. He had grown up with the century and loved all the inventions man was building to bend the world to his convenience. If the Wrights could build an airplane, Marconi a radio, and Ford a Model T, then certainly someone could build a sander that would free him from this drudgery. But there was no time to argue this morning because the promise the river had made at daybreak had now truly become a roar, distant yet, but no longer a sound describable in any other way.

Uncle Mac seemed not to hear. He opened another jar, swirled the paint, and studied the color. Jeremy glanced at him impatiently. The old man worked more slowly every day, studying longer between each cut with the chisel or stroke with the paintbrush.

Not that there was any reason to hurry. The furrier and the saddlemaker had placed their orders with Uncle Mac out of habit and friendship, not urgency. The bear's head and the horse's head might be the last orders Uncle Mac ever received, now that most shops advertised with signs rather than carved figures from McAlester's Woodcarving.

At thirteen, Jeremy could remember when nearly every shop on River Street had one of Uncle Mac's carvings hanging above its door. A giant hat hung over the milliner's, a bull's head over the butcher's, and a shoe over the shoemaker's. But no more. Even the wooden Indian that had stood for decades in front of Kelley's Cigar Store, a block over on Barstow, now leaned against the back wall of Uncle Mac's shop.

Outside, shopkeepers were leaving their stores to join the crowd hurrying to the foot of Porter Avenue to watch the log drive. Jeremy's father closed the door of Callahan's Sundries and came striding across the street, adjusting his new homburg hat. He pushed into the shop. "What, still here? The drive's just upstream."

"We'll be done in a minute," Uncle Mac said. "Young people don't understand patience," he muttered.

Mr. Callahan winked at Jeremy and Jeremy grinned; they'd heard it a hundred times. "Well, at least let your helper go."

"Patience. I'm almost done." Uncle Mac made a last careful stroke and sat for a moment gazing into the bear's eyes. "There," he said.

At the foot of Porter Avenue, the Chippewa ran high and fast, its waters swelled by the snowmelt and the heavy rains of a late spring. Jeremy spotted Willie and Eddie, the Cripshank twins, climbing a big maple to get the first sight of the drive as it rounded the bend. Uncle Mac leaned toward Jeremy and his father. "I would like to find a very good log today. People say that this is the last of the great drives. Thirty years ago a squirrel could jump from tree to tree clear across Wisconsin, but now the lumber companies have cut nearly all the pine."

"There'll always be logs for you to carve," Jeremy's father said.

"Yes, but there will be something special about a log from the last great drive."

"Here it comes!" Willie Cripshank yelled.

Jeremy dodged through the crowd to the maple. He scrambled up, joining Willie, Eddie, and three other boys in the branches. Out on the river, the first of the sixteen-foot pine logs bobbed and rolled in the current. Then in a rush the great pack of logs swung around the bend. Across the logs leaped the drivers—"river pigs" they called themselves. There wasn't a boy or a man in town who hadn't dreamed of being one of them: the toughest, the most daring of all the lumberjacks who worked in the pineries. Their voices rang in the May morning as they prodded and pushed with hooked peaveys and long pike poles to keep the logs moving straight downstream.

"Get that one, Joe."

"Bunching up back here."

"Watch that slippery devil."

"Har now, big fella, almost home."

With a "Keep 'em straight, boys," the drive boss birled a big log shoreward. "McAlester, you old coot!" he shouted. "Have I found a log for you! Sweetest stick I've ever ridden." He gestured downstream. "I'll beach 'er in the little bay this side of Valley One, and you can have a look."

Uncle Mac cupped his hands around his mouth. "I'll come. Don't lose her."

The drive boss waved. "Don't worry. I could pick 'er out of a million."

As the flood of logs smoothed into a steady stream, the crowd of spectators began to drift and then to break apart.

4

All through the day and on through the night, the river would carry the logs down to the mighty catch boom of monster chains and giant tree trunks strung across the river below the mills. There the Chippewa would slip from beneath, leaving its load behind, to flow on, unburdened, down the long miles to the Mississippi.

Jeremy's father hurried up the street to wait on the noon trade at Callahan's Sundries. Jeremy, Willie, and Eddie followed Uncle Mac across the Water Street Bridge and along a twisting, often-flooded lane by the river. The lane ended at the gravel beach left by the river in its final outward swing before the first of the mills.

The drive boss stood beside the beached log in the little bay, hands on hips, watching with satisfaction as his men brought the drive down to the catch boom. He turned, grinning. "And how is it with you, Mac?"

Uncle Mac shrugged. "Ah, I'm a year older and a year knottier, but among the living yet. And you, Ed?"

"Good, good. My last winter in the woods. We've finished the job, Mac. Cut nearly all the pine, God help us. But it was the job they paid us to do. Now I'll farm, add a child or two to the family, and feel grateful that the river never killed me."

"It's killed its share," Uncle Mac said. "Fetch me that peavey, Jeremy." The old man hefted the peavey and walked the length of the log, sounding the wood with the hook. "It's dry," he said. "Just the river water on her, but seasoned inside."

"Struck by lightning," the drive boss said. "You can see the scar."

The boys crowded in to examine the long gouge in the thick bark of the trunk. "Wow," Willie said. "Imagine getting hit by one of them lightning bolts? Bet it'd crack a guy's head right open."

"Not yours," Eddie said. "Probably just bounce off your thick head."

The drive boss pulled off a chunk of the bark. "Must've happened a year or two back. Else the bugs would have been at her. Altogether, she's a wonderment. Rode high and floated true, almost like she was in a hurry to get here."

Uncle Mac handed the peavey to Jeremy and sat on the log, running his big gnarled hands across the rough bark. "I know," he said. "I've been waiting for her."

Chapter 2

☽

The drive boss promised to send three of his drivers to load the log for the trip to Uncle Mac's shop. Uncle Mac thanked him and set off to hire a high-wheeled dray and a pair of workhorses. "You mind the log," he told Jeremy, handing him a quarter. "You can send your friends for sandwiches and sarsaparilla."

When Uncle Mac was out of earshot, Eddie said, "Why are you supposed to mind the log? It's not like anybody's going to walk off with a log."

Willie snorted. "Yeah, and I bet it wouldn't matter anyway. A log's a log. The next one'd be just as good."

"The next one wouldn't be seasoned," Jeremy said. "You can't carve until the tree's been dead a couple of years, or else the carving will split."

"Who cares?" Willie said. "Nobody needs that old junk anymore. Come on, give me a boost." He gave a swagger. "Ah'm gonna walk this stick like a river pig."

Jeremy locked his hands under Willie's bare foot and boosted him onto the log. Eddie followed, and together the twins reached down to help Jeremy up. Arms outspread for balance, they wobbled along the log, shouting warnings to one another about rapids and logjams, whirlpools, and rival crews.

Eddie gestured toward Water Street. "Who's going to the wanigan for chow?"

"I order you to go," Willie said, turning and tottering back toward him. "I'm the head push here."

"Says who?" Eddie snapped. "Nobody'd make you the bull driver. Not unless they were even dumber than you are."

Jeremy broke in before the twins could start pushing. "Hey, guys, I got the two bits and that makes me the head push here. And I say you both go."

Eddie glared at him. "Just like Westerhaus; you got the money, so you got the push."

"Hey, come on, Eddie," Jeremy said. "If you both go, one guy won't have to carry so much."

"Yeah, come on, Eddie," Willie said. "Ain't nothin' to fight about." He hopped off the log and started for Water Street. Eddie hesitated a moment before following, hands shoved in his pockets.

The twins came back with sandwiches and three bottles of sarsaparilla. The sandwiches were thick with cheese and meat, the sarsaparilla cold and sharp. They ate, watching the river, and then dozed in a warm patch of sun beneath the bank. Willie stretched. "Hey, Jeremy. How come your pa's never gotten married ag—*Ouch!* Hey, that hurt, Eddie!"

Eddie, who'd pinched him hard, growled, "Ain't your business to ask questions like that."

"What's the harm in askin'? Ain't we all friends?"

"Yeah, and maybe that's why you don't ask."

"It's all right," Jeremy said. "I don't mind." He stared up at the high blue of the sky, trying to remember his mother. "I guess he still misses my ma a lot. Like it isn't time yet."

"How long's it been?" Willie asked.

"Almost five years. Since I was eight."

"Wow, that's a long time," Willie said.

"Yeah," Eddie said. "Real long."

Jeremy felt the awkward pause and knew that they wanted to ask how it felt to lose a mother. But how could he explain? He hardly thought of his mother now, and when he did, he could only remember that small, shrunken someone who'd lain in the big bed in his parents' room, recognizing no one, while his father or Mrs. Higgins or Uncle Mac patiently spooned oatmeal into her slack mouth.

Yet telling that much would be the easy part, easier than explaining how the emptiness he'd felt then had begun to fill the day she'd drifted off into a death that was not that much different from the life she'd lived for years. Now when he saw his friends with their mothers, he never envied them, never wanted to trade places, because he had his father and Uncle Mac and only the smallest of holes remaining in his heart.

He jumped up before they could find the courage to ask any more questions. "I'm tired of sitting. Let's play hide-and-seek."

Eddie looked around. "Ain't much place to hide."

"Then let's play tag."

"I'll be it," Willie said.

They played tag until they tired of it, then combed the beach for anything valuable or strange brought down by the spring flood. They talked about what they would do now that school was out for the summer.

"Is your pa going to make you keep taking piano lessons?" Eddie asked.

Jeremy made a face, although secretly he enjoyed the piano more than he'd admit to anybody, particularly the Cripshank twins. "Yeah, and I've got to practice half an hour a day, too."

"Maybe you oughta try bein' poor like us." Willie laughed. "Ain't no way Pa'd buy us piano lessons. And if we had a piano, he'd carry it down to O'Sullivan's on his back and trade it for a bottle of the red-eye." He grinned at his own joke, and Eddie glowered at him.

"You guys gonna sell papers?" Jeremy asked.

Eddie shrugged. "Unless we can find something better." He brightened. "Think your pa might have a job for us?"

Jeremy shook his head. "Nah. He was complaining the other night that he's already got one stock boy too many in the warehouse. And you wouldn't want to work for Mr. Fitch in the store, believe me."

"I'd like to work with Arlyn behind the soda fountain," Willie said. "Get all the ice cream I could eat. Sarsaparilla, too."

"Like fudge!" Jeremy said. "He won't even let me have anything without a nickel or Pa's sayin' it's okay."

They fell silent, contemplating this unfairness. "So," Eddie said, "you gonna have to help your uncle carve this stick?"

Jeremy was already worried about that. "I don't know. I ain't promised to, but he might make me."

"Look!" Willie yelped.

Out on the river a driver had slipped, tumbling into the water amid the bumping, scraping logs. The boys held their breath until the driver's head and shoulders popped out of the water and he lunged onto a log, peavey still in hand. He was laughing as he balanced again, and the other drivers joined in, though only luck and muscle had saved him from a crushed arm or leg or even death.

Onshore the boys cheered. The driver grinned and lifted his peavey in salute, looking seven feet tall and at least half that wide across the shoulders. Another driver yelled: "Figured you for a goner, Dogan, but I was gonna grab your peavey. Give it to your widow to hang over the mantel."

"Ain't got no wife. I'm leaving everything to Wester-haus. I'm a company man."

"Son, old man Westerhaus bought your sorry hide the day you joined this outfit. That's why you'd be better off bein' a union man."

"Union talk," Eddie said. "Pa says it ain't nothin' but a bunch of claptrap the rabble-rousers use to get honest men's heads busted."

"Ah, forget that stuff," Willie said. "Let's play river pigs again. Give me a boost."

And remembering the best game of all, they clambered back atop the log and played at the escapes, tragedies, and triumphs of those who danced on the river.

The spring sun had grown pale and the afternoon cool by the time three drivers came strolling down the beach, two with peaveys and the third with a pike pole. They paused for a minute, and Jeremy caught a flash of sunlight on glass as something passed from hand to hand. "What are they doing?" he asked.

"Passing a pint of whiskey, stupid," Willie said, happy to call someone else stupid for a change.

"Temperance ladies see them, there'll be trouble," Eddie said. "A dozen of them were up and down Water Street last night, beating on a drum and telling the saloon owners how they should shut down before the drive got here."

"They were up on Barstow in the afternoon," Jeremy said. "They were trying to get people to sign a petition to make booze illegal. All of it, even beer."

Eddie snorted. "Not likely. Pa says the do-gooders can try to change the Constitution all they want, but they'll never get two things: the vote for women and prohibition. He says this is a Bible-believin' country and that it says right there in the Good Book that women are supposed to clayve to their husbands and leave the voting to them."

Willie bit his lip, but curiosity got the better of him. "What does he mean 'clayve'?"

"God, you're stupid," Eddie said. "Don't you remember how God made Adam out of clay?"

"Yeah, sure. But—"

"Well, women are supposed to remember that they weren't. That they got made out of Adam's rib. Or at least Eve was. So they're supposed to stick close to their husbands like, you know, a rib sticking in a hunk of clay. That's what clayve means."

Jeremy stared at Eddie and then asked, "Well, where's the Bible say that prohibition wouldn't be all right?"

Eddie gave him a superior look. "It don't say it right out, but it don't have to. In Genesis, God told Noah he could take a barrel of whiskey on the ark. And Pa says that means every workingman's got the God-given right to a snort of red-eye at the end of a hard day's work."

"Pa ought to know," Willie said. "He never misses his."

Jeremy was about to suggest that it really meant drinking was allowed only on big boats carrying loads of seasick animals through heavy rainstorms. But the drivers were again coming their way, and the three boys lost interest in politics and theology.

The biggest of the lumberjacks spoke. "This McAlester's stick?"

He really was very large, his heavy features made all the more frightening by a thick red beard. "Yes, sir," Jeremy gulped.

The three men laughed. "I ain't no 'sir,'" the man said. "Name's Murphy. Just plain Murphy. We're Brothers in Labor and we hate all that class talk. A man's a man or he ain't. These here are Sven and Soupy. And they are men for sure." He stuck out a huge, callused hand to Jeremy. "And what might you lads be called?"

They shook hands all around, and then the drivers made themselves comfortable against the bank. Sven, who was tall and blond, produced a short length of rope and began tying intricate knots, his strong fingers whipping loops and twists in the cord. Murphy watched indulgently. "Brother Sven was a fisherman in the old country. Now there ain't a top loader in the woods who can throw a timber hitch or a bowline faster. Ain't it so, Brother Sven?"

Sven nodded, unsmiling, although a faint blush came to his cheeks. "So I have been told."

Murphy smiled at the boys. "You boys know what a top loader is?" He explained how the top loader worked with chains, ropes, and pulleys to load the giant pine logs atop horse-drawn sleds for the trip through the winter woods to the riverbanks. "'Tis a hairy job, one that I leave to the likes of Sven."

The boys began asking questions, and soon Murphy and Sven were spinning tales about winters of forty below in the woods, roaring river drives in the spring, and a time not that long ago when the pines seemed to stretch forever. Murphy leaned back, relaxed in his storytelling, while Sven continued to weave his amazing knots. Soupy, the oldest, never spoke, but sat a little apart, seeming to enjoy the tales as much as the boys as he smiled and nodded with the remembering.

Murphy sighed. "Well, the Old Northwest is all finished up." His face darkened as he stared across the river at the roofs of the mansions built by Eau Claire's great lumbering families. "Over there's what it all built—all our sweat, frostbite, broken bones, and worse. It was the workingman who gave, but what'd he get?"

"Let it rest, Murph," Sven said. "You can get all riled up when we talk to those mill hands tomorrow night." He looked at the boys. "We got a little work to do around here, helping some of the boys get organized to demand a living wage and better hours. But after that we're gonna head for the New Northwest—Washington and Oregon and the big timber again."

Murphy brightened. "Heard tell the other day about some of them trees they call redwoods. Seems . . ."

The boys could have listened all day, but the rattle of harness and the creak of wooden wheels interrupted them. They turned to see Uncle Mac walking ahead of a four-wheeled dray drawn by two plodding workhorses. Lester, the Negro liveryman, grinned and waved.

Murphy stretched. "Time to float that stick, boys. Soupy, you go out and push open a spot. Sven and me'll get 'er moving your way. You lads keep a little back. I'll holler when I've got something for you to do."

Soupy sprang onto a log close to shore and jumped from it to the next until he was half a dozen logs into the pack. With his pike pole, he pushed and prodded the logs until he'd made space for Uncle Mac's log to float free of the shallows. Sven and Murphy locked their peaveys at opposite ends of the log and, with a heave, broke it loose from the gravel bottom.

"You've got her," Uncle Mac called. "Swing her butt end out and steady her while Lester brings the dray under."

While the drivers took places on logs to steady Uncle Mac's "stick," Lester brought the team around until the rear wheels of the dray lined up with the log. Jeremy knew Blanche and Jeanette, like he knew most of the dray horses along Water Street. A thousand times he'd seen them dragging loads patiently through the streets. Yet as powerful as the big horses were, Jeremy wondered if they could pull the great log out of the river and up the bank to the lane.

Lester seemed to have no doubt as he coaxed the team backward so that the dray edged under the floating log. The horses grew skittish when the river began lapping around their fetlocks, but Lester kept between their heads, speaking softly and patting their necks. Finally the log lay along the length of the dray. "All right, girls," Lester said, "easy now," and led them out of the water as the drivers pushed on the log and the dray took the load, until log, wagon, horses, and man came dripping from the river onto the beach.

Uncle Mac and Lester hammered block shims under the log to keep it from rolling. "Climb up," Lester called to the boys. "You straws won't make a nevermind to Blanche and Jeanette."

The boys cheered and scrambled onto the log. Blanche and Jeanette leaned into the harness and, with surprising ease, pulled the dray and log up the bank and onto the lane beyond.

The trip to Uncle Mac's shop became a parade, Murphy and Sven leading the way, Uncle Mac and Lester walking beside the horses, and Soupy bringing up the rear. People crowded out of shops and saloons to see. Already a number of lumberjacks were "spreeing" and yelled good-natured insults about some river pigs never knowing when to quit.

"Hey, McAlester," one of them called. "What you gonna carve out of that toothpick?" Uncle Mac acted like he hadn't understood and just waved.

At the edge of a crowd of lumberjacks, Jeremy saw fat Hans Weister, who called himself a businessman but was really only a bill collector. Weister raised his beer mug in mock salute. Eddie, whose family rented a ramshackle house from him, muttered something under his breath.

Mr. Callahan and a couple of the men from the warehouse met them at the shop. With a block and tackle, they helped Uncle Mac and the lumberjacks lift the butt end of the log. Lester snapped the reins, and Blanche and Jeanette pulled the dray out from under the other end, so that it fell with what was for the boys a disappointingly quiet thump. They cheered anyway, and even Uncle Mac smiled.

Chapter 3

☽

Jeremy loved the quiet of Callahan's at the end of the day, when his father locked the jingling door and drew down the shades over the big windows facing River Street. While Mr. Callahan and his clerk, Mr. Fitch, straightened up behind the counter and counted the till, Jeremy pushed the broom through the long, dim aisles with their smells of soap and talcum powder, cough syrup and liniment, chocolate and hard candy.

Callahan's Sundries also sold wholesale to stores in other towns, and two weeks a month, Jeremy's father took to the road to visit his customers. Uncle Mac kept an eye on the store then, although it really needed very little looking after, since Mr. Fitch and Arlyn, the soda-fountain man, knew the business as thoroughly as their employer.

Jeremy's father said good night to Mr. Fitch and then called to Jeremy, "Just about finished?"

"All done."

"Good. Put away your broom and let's go see what Mrs. Higgins made us for supper."

During the week, Mrs. Higgins left their supper on the stove before going home to look after her "mister." At the table, Mr. Callahan would prompt Jeremy to tell of his day. Then he would recount the news he'd heard in the store. Uncle Mac was rarely talkative, but he listened attentively, asking an occasional question. Tonight, he listened hardly at all. Finally, when Mr. Callahan got up to fetch the cherry pie from the oven, Uncle Mac spoke to Jeremy. "Tomorrow morning I'd like you to take a message to Nathan Two-Horse. You will have to memorize it, since I'm not sure he can read. Or if he can, whether he chooses to."

Jeremy stared at Uncle Mac. The old Chippewa Nathan Two-Horse lived far beyond the outskirts of town, and the idea of going all that way startled the plans he'd made for the morrow clear out of his head. He glanced at his father.

"Uncle Mac spoke to me. You're old enough to go on your own."

Jeremy felt his chest swell. "What do you want me to tell Two-Horse, Uncle Mac?"

"Tell him that I've come to understand why he knocked over the cigar-store Indian I carved for Kelley's and that I'm no longer angry. Then I want you to tell him that if he will come to see me, together we will make something beautiful."

"What are you going to carve?"

Uncle Mac hesitated. "A statue of a Chippewa maiden to honor his people and my craft before both are forgotten. But I'll talk to him about that. You just ask him to come."

At breakfast, Jeremy thought about asking Uncle Mac if he could take Willie and Eddie along. But that would be admitting that he was frightened to go alone, and he wouldn't admit that.

Mr. Callahan drew him a map, cautioned him twice about going too close to the rim of the flooded quarry he'd pass, and then went down to open the front door of Callahan's for the early trade. Uncle Mac drank the last of his coffee. "You remember what I told you to tell him?"

"Yes, sir," Jeremy said, and repeated the message.

Uncle Mac nodded. "Now Two-Horse may not agree to come right away. We had hard words all those years ago. But I know he is a curious man, and I think he will come eventually."

Jeremy could remember hearing about the incident but not the details. "Was Two-Horse drunk that night?"

"Yes, but there was more to it than that. There was something about my wooden Indian that angered him to rage. So he knocked it over."

"What happened then?"

"A constable arrested him and someone sent word to me that Kelley's wooden Indian had been destroyed. I went to look at it and the damage was bad, though not as bad as I'd been told. It was then, before the constable took him to jail, that I called Two-Horse some hard names that I still regret."

"What happened to him?"

"Judge Sorenson found him guilty of disturbing the peace and sent him to the county work farm for a month. But he was only there a few days before someone paid his fine and he went home."

"Who?"

"I suspect it was your father. He has a softer heart than is good for a man, although I have begun to understand that, too. Here, I packed a sandwich for you."

Jeremy climbed aboard the trolley, dropped his token in the box, and rode the clanging car to where the line ended at the foot of Menomonie Street. He was the only passenger by then, and the trolleyman gave him a curious look. "Know where you're going, son?"

"I'm walking to Nathan Two-Horse's. I've got a message for him."

The trolleyman raised bushy eyebrows. "That's a long way." He pointed toward the trolley shop on the far side of the street. "You'll want to start over there behind the repair building. Just follow the tracks where the old narrow-gauge railroad used to run to the quarry. There you'll pick up the path to the river. After that you're on your own."

"Does Two-Horse ride the trolley?"

"When he's got the fare. Says it's the only good thing the white man ever brought here." The trolleyman laughed. "Yep, that Two-Horse is quite the character. Mind that quarry. It's full of water and a lot deeper than you'd ever guess."

Jeremy followed the tracks of the narrow-gauge railroad that had once carried the sandstone blocks dug from the quarry before the deposit had grown too crumbly to mine. The quarry was a still place, without the flutter, song, and hum of birds and insects. Rain had seeped down through the ridge above, filling the depths with green water, flat and bottomless—or so it seemed when Jeremy threw a rock and watched it vanish a few inches below the surface as if dissolved to powder.

He was glad to keep to the tracks after that and happier still to turn onto the path to the river when he saw its blue shining through the scrub of maple and birch. He came out of the trees into high grass, where the path ambled along the bluff a hundred feet above the river. He looked upstream, making out the great catch boom that had broken the rush of logs. At this distance he could not make out the individual logs, yet it seemed that the gray surface rippled ever so slightly, the logs bobbing patiently as the current slid beneath.

He walked along the bluff for the better part of an hour before pausing where the path swung inland toward the wooded ridge where Nathan Two-Horse's shanty stood. He found a spot on a sunny boulder and ate his lunch, though it was early yet and he knew that he would be hungry on the way back.

He rehearsed the message while he ate, then set off for the ridge, whose slopes had grown thick with maple and birch in the years since the lumber companies had cut the pine from the country around Eau Claire. The trail narrowed to a bare trace in the brush, and Jeremy felt his heart constrict with the fear that he would never find

Two-Horse's cabin—or that if he did, it would be too menacing for any white boy to approach. But then the trail broke into a sunny wash of cleared ground against the foot of the ridge and he saw Two-Horse's shanty.

Jeremy hesitated in the shadow of one of the few pines he'd seen all day—a wolf tree too limby and twisted to attract the loggers' saws and axes. From the moment he'd set out, he'd pictured himself marching to Two-Horse's door and delivering his message through a door cracked by the silent old Indian. But Two-Horse was in his garden, hoeing freshly planted rows of corn. He was intent on his work, and it wasn't until he reached the end of a row that he looked up and saw Jeremy. His lined dark face betrayed neither surprise nor hostility in the instant before he smiled. "Hello, boy. Are you lost?"

Jeremy cleared his throat. "Uh, no, sir. My uncle, that is, my great-uncle, Dan McAlester, sent me to give you a message. He said to tell you . . ." And he plunged in, trying to remember all that he had so carefully memorized but that now seemed suddenly fragile in the remembering.

Two-Horse listened, and when Jeremy finished, stood silent a moment before saying, "Come. It's hot, and I have good water here."

Under the overhang of the shanty's roof, Two-Horse dipped cold, clear water from a pail into a tin cup and handed it to Jeremy. Jeremy sipped, then drank, surprised at his sudden thirst. Two-Horse refilled the cup, filled another for himself, and then gestured Jeremy to a seat on a rough pine bench while he squatted in the shade across from him.

"It is very good water," Jeremy said. "It doesn't taste of iron like city water. I guess because it doesn't come through pipes."

Two-Horse smiled faintly. "No, no pipes." He pointed toward the ridge. "It's from a spring up there. The animals come to drink and so do I."

Jeremy waited for him to say more, but Two-Horse seemed to have fallen into thought, his gaze fixed on some point far distant in time. Finally, when Jeremy couldn't bear the silence any longer, he asked, "What should I tell Uncle Mac? Will you come?"

Two-Horse sipped from his cup. "I have to hoe my garden. Then maybe I will come." He shrugged, laughter crinkling the corners of his eyes. "Or maybe not. It's hard to know with Indians."

Chapter 4

☽

Nathan Two-Horse did not come the next day, nor the day after that. "Does that mean he's not coming?" Jeremy asked Uncle Mac on the morning of the third day as the two of them worked in the carving shop.

"No, it just means that the spirit hasn't moved him yet. If he doesn't come in a week, I'll start worrying." Uncle Mac ran his hand over the horse's head from nose to neck. "A little here beneath the jaw and it will be smooth enough."

Jeremy had never heard more welcome words. His hands were sore, his arms ached, and he was bored almost to madness. For another half hour, he sanded furiously. "After dinner," he called to Uncle Mac, "Willie, Eddie, and I thought we'd try Half Moon for crappies."

"All right," Uncle Mac said. "But help me hang Edson's bear first. It will only take a few minutes."

"Sure," Jeremy said, relieved that Uncle Mac wasn't expecting him to spend the afternoon helping to paint the horse's head.

But then Uncle Mac went on. "Tomorrow we'll start peeling the log, whether Two-Horse comes or not. Next day we'll saw the piece to carve. Two big days."

Jeremy felt his heart sag. He had so many plans for the summer days ahead! But now it seemed that Uncle Mac expected him to help carve the Chippewa maiden—all because he'd volunteered to sand the horse's head on a rainy Saturday afternoon in April when summer seemed far away.

The big crappies in Half Moon Lake wouldn't bite that afternoon, and no boy with any self-respect would carry a mess of the small ones home through the streets of the West Side. When Jeremy came into Callahan's to sweep, he was grumpy with sunburn and disappointment. Mr. Callahan was behind the soda-fountain counter, helping Arlyn inventory glasses and dishes. "Fish for supper?" he called.

"Not unless you caught some."

"No, can't say I got away. Need something cold to buck up the spirits before work?"

Jeremy hesitated. "I guess a Coca-Cola might help."

Mr. Callahan dipped shaved ice into a glass and filled it with the brown, almost black soda. "You know," he said, "when I was your age, they sold this as medicine. It wasn't a drink people paid money to enjoy."

"Yeah, you told me. About a thousand times, too."

His father tousled Jeremy's hair. "Just don't want you to forget." Jeremy shrugged away and pushed the hair from his eyes.

Arlyn finished counting a row of dishes beneath the counter and straightened his long, angular frame. "And nineteen of the old sundae dishes. That's everything, Mr. Cal. If you don't need me anymore, I'll be on my way."

"That's fine. We'll see you in the morning." Mr. Callahan finished adding the columns of figures. "So," he asked, "no fish at all?"

Jeremy shrugged. "We got a few little ones, but nothing worth keeping. I'd go back in the morning if I could. I know we'd catch fish if we got there early. But Uncle Mac says I've got to help him peel the log."

Mr. Callahan leaned against the back counter. "And you don't want to help."

Jeremy shifted uncomfortably. "Well, it's not exactly that, Pa. But I don't want to spend all summer sitting in his stupid shop. I don't do anything important, anyway. Just sand and fetch and listen to him talk about how things were better before we had all the new machines."

Mr. Callahan considered. "Well, there are many boys your age who have to work a lot harder. Even with the new labor laws, many children still work in mines and mills."

"I know, Pa, but—"

Mr. Callahan held up a palm. "Hold on. I agree that you shouldn't spend the whole summer working. But a little work never hurt a boy. Now I can put you to work here, helping Fitch stock shelves a few hours a day, or you can help Uncle Mac in his shop."

Jeremy grimaced. He liked the store better than the shop, but Mr. Fitch was even crankier than Uncle Mac. "I guess I'll help Uncle Mac carve his stupid statue."

"Personally, I think you'd have more fun, and it'll probably be your last chance to see anyone carve something that size. I think he'll close up the shop when he's done. You may think he's old-fashioned, but he won't hold on to something when he knows its time has passed. But it's not going to be easy for him, and that's why I think he wants you to keep him company this last time. . . . Say, did you hear they're having balloon rides at the fair on the Fourth of July?"

"Balloons are nineteenth century. I'd rather ride in an airplane."

His father laughed. "Well, someday maybe you will. But come now. Wouldn't you like to ride in a balloon? Be up there in the clouds with the birds?"

"Sure, but I don't have the money saved for any balloon rides."

"Well, you leave that worry to me. Just pay attention to Uncle Mac, remember to practice the piano every day as your mother would have liked, and together we'll have a grand time at the fair." He grinned. "And I'll throw in a quarter a day if you can do both with a smile." He stuck out a hand. "Fair enough?"

And with the image of floating through the clouds gaining real possibility in his imagination, Jeremy grasped the proffered hand. His father held the grip for a moment. "Have you still got that ten-dollar gold piece your mother left you?"

"Sure."

"Good. I've told you all along that you needn't save it for her sake, but it's always good to have something laid by."

* * *

That evening Jeremy hurried through his piano practice, hoping that his father wouldn't notice his haste. Down on the river, the fish would be biting along the edge of the logs in the dusk. The sun was brushing the stacks of the sawmills on the far side of the river when Jeremy crossed River Street. He took the spade from beside the shop and hurried around back to dig for worms. There, in the dimming light, he nearly stumbled into Nathan Two-Horse.

The old Chippewa sat on a rickety sawhorse, fingering a peeled willow stick. He turned, as unsurprised as before at Jeremy's sudden appearance. "Hello, boy."

Startled, it took Jeremy a moment to summon his manners. "Hello, sir," he managed.

Two-Horse pointed with the stick at the cigar-store Indian leaning against the back wall of the shop, its rain-washed eyes staring vacantly at the river. "Has it been here long?" he asked.

"Since last fall, when Mr. Kelley told Uncle Mac he didn't want it anymore."

Two-Horse considered this, then rose. "See where I broke its head off?" He traced a faint crack on the neck of the statue with the stick.

"Yes."

He turned to look at Jeremy, his eyes shadowed, the stick lying like a knife across the throat of the carved Indian. "Did your great-uncle tell you why I did it?"

"I'm not sure that he . . . well, that he really knows."

"You said that he did when you came to my cabin."

"Yes, but . . . Well, he never told me if he does."

"Would you like to know?"

"Uh . . . sure. If you'd like to tell me."

Two-Horse stepped closer to the Indian so that they stood eye to eye, wooden and beating chests almost touching. "I was drunk. Drunk and staggering down the street like a fool when I came upon this painted *thing*." He spat the word. "This wooden Indian made by a white man for another white man to sell what for us had been a sacred plant, but that white men made into just another of their filthy habits."

He fell silent, his face nearly touching the carved face. Jeremy wondered if he was even aware of him any longer. Perhaps if he took a step backward and then another . . .

Two-Horse laughed. "So, boy, I knocked over your great-uncle's stupid statue. And if I hadn't been so drunk, I'd have smashed it to pieces. But I was still staggering around, trying to find a board or a rock, when the constable caught me." He shrugged. "And all that matters about the rest of it you already know." He stared at Jeremy. "Since that night I've never tasted the white man's whiskey. Not because I am ashamed of what I did, but because I was finished with drinking his poison. Do you understand?"

Jeremy nodded. Suddenly, in a motion almost too quick for the eye, Two-Horse tossed him the polished stick. Jeremy caught it by reflex, finding it light, almost unbelievably smooth. Two-Horse chuckled. "They say my grandfather could change one of those into a snake in midair. Do you believe that?" Jeremy held the stick a little away from him, then shook his head. Two-Horse smiled. "No, I'm not sure I do, either, but it's better not to take chances." He reached out and took the stick. "Tell your great-uncle that we will talk in the morning. If he has coffee, that would be good."

Mr. Callahan and Uncle Mac listened while Jeremy told them of his meeting with Two-Horse. And to his surprise, Jeremy felt his voice quaver. "He scared me. The other day out at his cabin he didn't frighten me at all. I thought he was real nice then. But tonight he was different."

The two men exchanged glances. Mr. Callahan cleared his throat. "He wouldn't hurt you, Jeremy. I've known Two-Horse all my life, and drunk or sober, he'd never hurt a child."

"You're sure he wasn't drinking?" Uncle Mac asked.

"Well, not sure sure. I mean, he said he wasn't, and I didn't smell anything."

"That's good. Then he will come in the morning."

"Uncle Mac, do you think that his grandpa could really change a willow stick into a snake?"

Uncle Mac considered for longer than Jeremy liked. "Well, in the Bible, Moses cast his staff on the earth and it turned into a serpent. But, no, I don't think Two-Horse's grandfather could turn a willow stick into a snake."

Mr. Callahan spoke. "Jeremy, these are superstitions. Things from the old days. Two-Horse himself doesn't believe the story. He all but told you that. His grandfather may have known a trick, and it may have been a very good one, but it was a trick. Tonight Two-Horse just had a little fun with you."

"Why?" Jeremy asked.

"Perhaps to show you that people and things aren't always quite what they seem. Maybe that's what his grandfather taught with his trick, however he did it."

Chapter 5

☽

Jeremy was coming down the steps from his piano teacher's studio when Two-Horse rose from his seat by the log, nodded to Uncle Mac, and limped up the street. At the trolley stop, he waited patiently until the car came clanging around the corner.

"Where's he going, Uncle Mac?" Jeremy asked. "That's not the way home."

"He's going to see somebody on the North Side. A niece or a great-niece. I'm not sure which."

"Is she at the convent school?"

"No, she works for a milliner. She was at the convent school, studying to be a teacher, but Two-Horse says she's given that up to make hats."

"Why? Isn't being a teacher better?"

Uncle Mac sighed. "Nancy Two-Horse would rather make hats than leave the city. If she becomes a teacher, no school will hire her except on one of the reservations."

"Well, I don't think I'd want an Indian for a teacher. I mean, they did fight us, didn't they?"

Uncle Mac shook his head. "Two-Horse's people never fought the whites. Not really. The Chippewa tried to get along and lost nearly everything in the bargain. But even if they had, what difference should that make now?"

Jeremy looked down. "I guess you're right."

Uncle Mac grunted. "It's happened. Not as often as I would have liked in my life, but now and then." He picked up the pot beside his chair and poured the last of it into his cup.

"I can understand why she'd rather stay here, though," Jeremy said. "I wouldn't want to live way out in the woods where nothing ever happens. Heck, even Two-Horse doesn't live on the reservation. He'd rather be somewhere where he can ride the trolley."

Uncle Mac sipped from his cup, made a face, and poured the cold coffee on the ground. "He doesn't stay for the trolley cars. He has other reasons."

"What?"

"To watch, now that our time is passing." He rose before Jeremy could ask another question. "Let's eat. Then we'll sharpen the barking spuds and start peeling the log."

Jeremy hurried to keep up with Uncle Mac's long strides as they crossed the street. "What did Two-Horse say about helping?"

"He said he would, but only if I made her the Chippewa way. With respect."

"What'd you say?"

"I told him now that I've grown old, I've forgotten any other way." Uncle Mac chuckled. "And he said that I would have made a good politician. So we understand each other. But perhaps two old liars can make something beautiful despite themselves."

* * *

Uncle Mac scored the bark with an ax, and the two of them stood side by side on the log, working the chisel blades of the long-handled spuds under the bark until it came loose in chunks. In an hour Jeremy's hands began to blister. Uncle Mac gave him gloves, but before long his palms stung through the leather.

"That's enough," Uncle Mac said. "You can start picking up the bark."

Jeremy stacked the chunks of bark against the side of the shop, where they would dry under the eaves until fall and the time to light the fire in the barrel stove. Uncle Mac worked steadily at the log, peeling away the gray bark to reveal the white wood beneath. Finally, the log lay bare from end to end. Uncle Mac leaned his spud against it and wiped his face with a bandanna. "It's beautiful wood," he said. "Clear and straight. It will make a beautiful statue."

"Which end are you going to use?"

"Neither. We're going to use the center from here to here." He measured out a length of about eight feet.

Jeremy stared. "That big?"

"Part of it will be cut away at the end of the carving, but the maiden's going to be life-size. And I understand that Nancy Two-Horse is a tall girl."

Jeremy looked at him questioningly.

Uncle Mac shrugged. "I hadn't meant to tell you until I was certain, but if Two-Horse can convince her, we'll use Nancy as the model. He says she's very pretty."

"When is she coming?"

"Tomorrow, I hope."

In the morning, they delivered the horse's head to Mr. Renard, the saddlemaker, and helped him hang it over the door of his shop. Uncle Mac and his old friend stood back to admire the head, but Jeremy found himself disappointed. He had spent days sanding it, but now the head hung so high that even those who bothered to pause would never see how smooth his hands had made the wood.

Back at the shop, Uncle Mac laid the long crosscut saw on the bench and carefully filed each of the teeth. Jeremy shifted on his stool, impatient with the wait. "No time is ever lost in sharpening," Uncle Mac said. "Sharp tools make fast work."

Outside, he studied the log a final time, selected a spot, and drew the saw across so that the teeth bit in and held the blade. He gestured Jeremy to the other handle. "Now remember," he said, "draw, never push. Pull it your way, relax and let me draw it back my way, and then draw again." Jeremy bit his lip and nodded.

In the first few minutes, he forgot several times and pushed on his end so that the saw bowed and jerked. Each time Uncle Mac said patiently, "Draw, relax, let me draw it back. You're getting it."

Steadily, almost without realizing it, Jeremy found the rhythm. Uncle Mac picked up the speed until the saw sang through the wood. Watching the blade flashing back and forth, Jeremy lost track of time. Finally, when they were halfway through, Uncle Mac called out, "One, two, three, and stop."

Jeremy stepped back, his ears and muscles still singing. Uncle Mac put a hand against the small of his back and straightened with a grunt. "You're built better for this than I am. Closer to the ground and a lot more limber. How are your hands?"

Jeremy took off his gloves and looked. "Fine. One blister, but I think that's from yesterday."

"Born to be a sawyer," Uncle Mac said.

They got a drink of water and went back to the sawing. Jeremy said, "I could get Willie and Eddie to give us a hand this afternoon. I bet they'd love a chance to saw with a real crosscut."

"All right. You'll make a good teacher."

Willie and Eddie were blaming each other for binding the saw when Jeremy looked up and saw Two-Horse and a girl of seventeen or eighteen coming down the street. "Hey, who's that with Two-Horse?" Eddie asked.

"That must be his niece," Jeremy said. "She works for a milliner up on the North Side."

"I never knew he had any relatives," Willie said. "I thought he was the last of his tribe."

"Uncle Mac says there are lots of Chippewa up by Hayward," Jeremy said.

"That Two-Horse's tribe? I always thought he was something different. You know, a Mohican or something."

"They all died," Eddie said. "Ma read *The Last of the Mohicans* to us, remember? Criminy, you're stupid."

Jeremy let them argue while he studied Two-Horse's niece. She was tall for a Chippewa girl—taller than Two-

Horse—and pretty, but her face had a sullen look and she seemed to be following the old man reluctantly.

Uncle Mac came out of the shop to greet them. Nancy gave one quick bob of her head and stared at the ground. "Come in," Uncle Mac said. "I have coffee."

"Let's listen," Eddie hissed.

He should have stopped them, but Jeremy very much wanted to hear. They scuttled to the half-open window and crouched beneath it. Two-Horse was speaking: "Nancy says she can come in the late afternoon after she is done making hats. I will find the proper clothes for her." The boys heard Nancy say something softly in Chippewa.

Uncle Mac hesitated. "How well does she speak English?"

"Better than you do," Two-Horse said. "And she knows many other things. Enough to be a teacher. But she put all that away to make hats for rich white women. So maybe she is ashamed now and won't speak English in front of a white man."

Nancy spoke angrily in a low voice, a stream of words in Chippewa that seemed to shut Two-Horse up. For a couple of minutes, no one spoke. Jeremy glanced at the log nervously. There was still a foot and a half of the second cut to go, and soon Uncle Mac would notice that the saw no longer sang in the yard.

It was Nancy who spoke first, this time in English. "Uncle wants me to do this thing. I would rather not, but I was raised to obey my elders like any good Chippewa girl. So I will come."

Uncle Mac cleared his throat. "Miss Two-Horse, I will pay—"

"No," Nancy said. "You can pay my trolley fare."

"Of course," Uncle Mac said.

Two-Horse and Nancy had another quick exchange in Chippewa. Two-Horse was emphatic. He spoke to Uncle Mac. "You may carve how Nancy stands and what she wears, but do not put her face on the statue. That would be threatening her spirit. The nuns have told her not to believe such things, but I still believe."

"Then how will I know what face to carve?" Uncle Mac asked.

"Something will tell you or it won't. If it doesn't, then you've lied to me and the statue won't matter."

There was a long pause. The boys heard Uncle Mac's chair creak as he rose to pour more coffee. They scuttled back to the saw.

A few minutes later Uncle Mac called Jeremy's name. He hurried to the front door of the shop. "Jeremy, I want you to meet Two-Horse's niece, Nancy," Uncle Mac said. "Nancy, this is my great-nephew, Jeremy."

When he met her dark eyes, Jeremy's heart did a sudden, startling skip. He gulped. "Pleased to meet you."

A faint smile lifted a corner of her mouth. "Thank you, Jeremy. I am pleased, too."

He reddened, fearing that he had given away what had troubled him since he'd first seen her coming down the street a step behind Two-Horse.

Chapter 6

☽

A loud knocking downstairs interrupted their dressing for church on Sunday morning. Jeremy watched from the landing as his father opened the door to a flush-faced Mrs. Jensen, owner of Jensen's Boardinghouse and Travelers' Inn. "Mr. Callahan! I want you to know the shameful, unchristian goings-on I saw over by Mr. McAlester's shop this morning. That savage, Two-Horse, was there, shaking a rattle, scattering some sort of red powder, and conducting Lord knows what manner of heathen sacrifice over the log that black man and those lumberjacks brought up from the river last week."

"Now, now, Mrs. Jensen. I'm sure—"

"Mr. Callahan, this is a Christian community! Why, what if the children saw?"

"Mrs. Jensen, I know this is a Christian community. Right now we're dressing for church. And I'm sure that if you were to ask, you would find that Two-Horse is a Christian, too. But he has his traditions as we have ours. . . ."

Mr. Callahan stepped onto the porch, closing the door behind him, and Jeremy couldn't make out their muffled words. He hurried down the last few steps to watch his father gently guiding Mrs. Jensen across the sidewalk. At first, she seemed as huffed up as an irate prairie chicken, but by the time they had crossed the street, Jeremy could see that his father's charm had smoothed her almost to normal size and that she was smiling and preening in the glow of his attention.

"Another victory for Irish stuff and nonsense," Uncle Mac said behind him.

"Did you hear what she said?" Jeremy asked.

Uncle Mac snorted. "Who couldn't hear the squawking of that old biddy? Half the street probably heard."

"Does it bother you what Two-Horse did?"

"Two-Horse shook a rattle, scattered some powder, and said a prayer. Why should that bother me? I don't have to believe what he believes, and he can believe what he wants to believe. And, as far as that goes, so can Roberta Jensen. I haven't paid any attention to her in the last forty years and I don't plan to start now."

Jeremy's father came back into the store, laughing. "Come on, men. Let's get to church. Mother Jensen already suspects we're in league with the devil, and you can bet we'll suffer the consequences if we don't show our faces among the faithful."

Jeremy rose early on Monday morning to ride with his father to the train station. When they brought the last of the sample cases down to the street, Lester was waiting with a buggy hitched behind Iris, a mare they often hired. "Want me to come along, Mr. Cal, or can young Jeremy bring Iris back safely?"

Mr. Callahan looked at Jeremy. "What do you think?"

"I can handle her, Pa. She knows me."

"He'll be all right, Lester. Thanks for coming out so early."

Mr. Callahan handed him a half dollar, and Lester touched his hat. "My pleasure, Mr. Cal. Have a good trip."

In the buggy Jeremy said, "Pa, a whole fifty cents?"

Mr. Callahan shrugged. "Lester probably doesn't make much more a day, though he's as good a man as any white man you'll ever meet. I can afford to make up a little for the unfairness. Mind the reins now."

They crossed the Eau Claire River on the Barstow Street Bridge, a few hundred yards upstream of the point where the smaller river emptied into the Chippewa. As they rattled on into the North Side, Jeremy heard a train whistle in the distance, and though he knew there was no real hurry, he flicked the reins and clucked so that Iris broke into an easy trot.

The chuffing engine had barely stopped when a porter swung down from the Pullman car. "Morning, Mr. Cal. Where are we off to today?"

"Good morning, Raymond. Off to Chicago to do some buying. Then a little selling on the way back."

"Looks to be a lot of selling. How many cases we got here?"

"Five and my bag. They all have tags."

Raymond bustled off with two of the heavy cases. "Are all the porters Negroes, Pa?" Jeremy asked.

"I believe so. And all the conductors are white. But that will change. Well, I'd better find a seat. After Chicago, I'm

41

going to Fond du Lac, Appleton, Wisconsin Rapids, Wausau, and a few smaller places in between. I'll be back in two weeks, maybe a day or two short of that if everything goes well." He hesitated and then, rather than embracing Jeremy, he extended a hand. "Thanks for bringing me, son. Look after things."

Jeremy took his hand awkwardly. "Sure, Pa. You be careful."

On the way back to the livery stable, Jeremy minded the reins with exaggerated care until Iris shook her head to let him know that he could still trust her. They recrossed the Eau Claire and clopped down Barstow. The long main street of the business district had only begun to stir and they traveled its length without having to slow for buggies, wagons, or automobiles. They turned off on Emery Street and pulled up in front of the livery stable.

Lester turned from hitching Blanche and Jeanette to their dray. "Get him off in style, Jeremy?"

"Sure did. And Iris was just fine on the way back."

Lester slapped her haunch. "Yes, she's a good girl. So what's Mr. Mac carving out of that big log Blanche, Jeanette, and me helped him move?"

"I'm not really supposed to tell, but I think he'd tell you if you asked."

Lester laughed. "Oh, it's a secret then. Well, I don't much concern myself with secrets unless they come to me natural. And then I don't repeat 'em. That's why Mr. Weister don't like me, because I never tell him anything I overhear. He ever try to give you a nickel for a secret?"

"A couple of times, but I didn't take it. Some of the other kids take pennies and nickels for telling him things, but I don't like him."

"Nobody likes Mr. Weister. It's just that some people pay attention to him. I don't." Lester winked.

Murphy, the big, red-haired lumberjack, came to the shop soon after breakfast. His face was puffy and his eyes red from a night of spreeing on Water Street, but he smiled at Jeremy. "Morning, lad. Got this stick all peeled for me?"

"Yes, sir."

"Well, let me cadge a cup of your uncle's blackjack and then I'll see what I can do. And, remember, I ain't no 'sir.' Just a Brother in Labor."

Jeremy knew Uncle Mac would never hurry a man with his coffee, so he climbed into the maple tree beside the shop. Below on the river, the pack of logs looked as thick as ever despite the saws of the mills whining day and night to cut the lumber. It saddened him to hear that the pine was nearly gone. All his life he'd heard of the great forest and now he'd never see it for himself.

Uncle Mac called his name.

"Up here, Uncle Mac."

"Come and help me set the dogs before Mr. Murphy starts squaring the log."

Jeremy scrambled down. Uncle Mac handed him a pair of tongs and the long metal stake called a hewing dog. Jeremy held the stake in place with the tongs while Uncle Mac drove it into the ground with a short-handled sledgehammer until the claw head of the hewing dog bit deep into the wood.

While they secured both ends of the log, Murphy sat astride the bench by the wall to sharpen a double-bitted ax and a ferocious broadax. Jeremy knew that Uncle Mac would already have a good edge on both, but like every lumberjack, Murphy would put on the fine edge himself. The big man touched a thumb to the twelve-inch blade of the broadax. "Now a normal man could shave with this, but my fine Irish skin is a bit too sensitive. So I'll waste my nickel on the barber." He laid it aside, picked up the double-bitted ax, and strolled to the log. He paused, studying it. "And what is this red powder on the wood?"

"It's nothing that matters," Uncle Mac said. "Just an old Indian's custom."

Murphy frowned. "Heathen superstition?" To Jeremy's surprise, the big lumberjack actually looked uncertain for a moment. But then he grinned. "Ah, well. The devil contracted for my soul long ago, I fear. Stand back, lads."

He hopped nimbly onto the log, the calks on his boots biting into the wood. He stood crosswise, spat on his hands, weighed the ax for a moment, then swung. The blade bit into the side of the log. He raised the ax again, the handle spinning in his hand so that the opposite blade drove into the wood, sending a big chip flying away from the log. He grunted with satisfaction, shifted his position a little to set the calks of his boots, and began swinging quick rhythmic strokes.

"Why does he switch blades?" Jeremy asked Uncle Mac. "Why doesn't he just use one until it's dull and then switch to the other one?"

"They're honed differently. One cuts and releases best to the right, the other to the left. Watch now. There won't be men like Murphy around much longer."

The chips flew as Murphy scored both sides of the log at intervals of a foot. When he'd finished, Jeremy brought him the broadax. Murphy grinned down at him, looking as tall as Paul Bunyan from his perch on the log. "The ol' wood straightener's a mite heavy, eh?"

"Yes, s—Uh, brother."

"There you've got it." His grin widened. He reached down to take the handle of the broadax in a huge hand.

Murphy swung the broadax lengthwise with the log, the blows tearing away huge chips between the scoring cuts he'd made with the double-bitted ax. Sometimes the razor edge of the blade came within an inch of his boot, but never closer. His face was red now and running with sweat, but he didn't pause until he had squared the first side of the log.

By then a small crowd had gathered in the street. When Murphy hopped down to get a drink from the water bucket, a couple of the young men who clerked at the bank began cajoling Uncle Mac to tell what he planned to carve. "You'll see in good time," Uncle Mac said, and tried to ignore them.

But they wouldn't be ignored and began talking loudly about "nineteenth-century nonsense."

"All right," Murphy called, climbing back on the log. "A little quiet, if you please, for the boyo swinging the big ax." He stared at the two young men, who suddenly seemed to remember that their dinner hour was nearly over and hastened from the crowd. Murphy winked at Jeremy.

45

The crowd shifted, old faces replaced by fewer new ones, until it wasn't a crowd at all but only the occasional passerby or two pausing to watch Murphy swinging the broadax. Willie and Eddie Cripshank watched for a while, then took places on the bench against the wall and began playing mumblety-peg. It was only when Jeremy turned to watch the game that he noticed Two-Horse squatting in the shadows behind the shop.

Murphy finished squaring the second side. Uncle Mac knocked the hewing dogs free and together the two men turned the log with cant hooks. Walking now on a squared side, Murphy no longer had to worry about his footing and the work went faster. Uncle Mac handed Jeremy a nickel. "Fetch a pail of beer from the hotel. Mr. Murphy will be thirsty."

"He doesn't like being called 'sir' or 'mister.' He says none of the Brothers in Labor like fancy talk."

Uncle Mac studied Murphy with new interest. "That means he's a union man, like some of the mill hands, though they can't admit to it. Well, more power to him. Someone has to fight the big companies. Now go quickly; he'll be done soon."

Jeremy got the clean covered pail from the shop and, with Eddie and Willie trailing along, hurried to the hotel. The taproom was dark and cool, smelling of leather, beer, and cigar smoke. A few businessmen were finishing late lunches from the trays of cold cuts, cheeses, breads, and pickles laid out on a table against the far wall. They only glanced at the boys before returning to their conversations and meals. The bartender filled the pail, his big arm working the handle of the pump that drew the frothing beer from the keg. "Five cents, boys. Unless you plan to drink it here, then I'll have to charge you another nickel."

A man down the bar chuckled. Now that his eyes had adjusted to the gloom, Jeremy recognized Hans Weister. "Go ahead and give 'em three sarsaparillas on me, Bill. Then young Callahan can tell me what that crazy old coot McAlester is doing with that log."

Jeremy shoved the nickel across the bar. "No thanks, Mr. Weister. Uncle Mac told us to get right back."

Outside, Eddie said, "Criminy, we could've stayed for a sarsaparilla, Jeremy. How long's that take?"

"Too long with him. He just wants to know what's none of his business."

"Let's sneak a swallow of the beer," Willie said. "Beer ain't so bad. Not so good as sarsaparilla, but it ain't bad."

"How would you know?" Jeremy asked.

The twins looked at each other and laughed. "We know," Eddie said. "Pa don't always make it through the pail he buys on his way home from work, especially if he hangs around O'Sullivan's for an hour or two. Then you can be sure he ain't gonna make it through the pail. So we help out."

"Come on," Willie said. "Let's go back in the alley and have a pull."

"No, we gotta hurry," Jeremy said.

"We can always tell Weister how Nancy Two-Horse is going to model for a statue of a beyoutiful Injun girl," Eddie said.

Willie gave his snorting laugh. "Beyouuuutiful."

Jeremy hesitated, then let them pull him into the alley, where the twins each took a long swallow from the pail. Jeremy clapped the cover back on before they could take another. "That's enough. You guys will get drunk!"

"Ha," Willie said. "Takes more than that to get us drunk."

Murphy had squared the log into a rough beam, and he sat on it now, wiping his red face with a bandanna. "Ah," he said, "here are my lads." He took the pail, tossed the cover to Jeremy, and took a long draft of the beer. He sighed, belched, and extended the pail to Uncle Mac.

"No, you've earned it, Brother Murphy. I'll wait until supper for my beer."

Murphy crossed his legs and began working at the pail. "So your nephew told you I was a Brother in Labor, eh?"

"He did."

"And what say you to that?"

"I say it's high time working folk had a voice."

Murphy stared at his big, scarred hands, which made the pail seem small in their hold. "Sometimes I think we have too many voices," he said. "We need to speak as one. But that will come. Already they say that the men in lumber camps in the New Northwest are fighting for their rights. I am looking forward to seeing it."

"When are you going?" Jeremy asked.

"Soon, lad. As soon as old Westerhaus lays on a train to take us there. He'll try to keep us union boys off, but we'll go anyway." He took another long drink from the pail and grinned. "Say, you lads ain't going to make me do all the work, are you? Fetch the auger and you can start drilling holes in the ends of what's left of this stick."

Uncle Mac told Jeremy which auger to bring, then went to measure where to drill the holes in the ends of the beam. Murphy finished the pail of beer and stretched out on the bench by the wall, cap over his eyes.

When Willie and Eddie leaned in to watch Uncle Mac set the auger, he sniffed the air. "Have you boys been drinking beer?"

"No, sir," they said in unison, pulling back too quickly to be believed.

Uncle Mac looked hard at Jeremy. "I didn't drink any," Jeremy said.

Uncle Mac stared at the Cripshank twins. "I ought to tell your grandmother. Nobody at your house may care, but she'd take a switch to the both of you." The twins nodded dumbly. "Are you going to behave around here?" They nodded. "All right then. Mind you do."

When Uncle Mac had the auger set in the wood an inch, the angle to his satisfaction, he rose and went into the shop. "Do you think he'll tell?" Willie asked.

"No," Jeremy said. "But he'll remember. I wouldn't give him any excuses to tell on you later on."

"Like what excuse?" Eddie said.

"Like telling Weister or somebody else what he's going to carve. That'd get him real angry. And don't forget, I can tell how you finish off your pa's beer when he falls asleep."

The twins exchanged glances. "We won't tell," Eddie said.

"No sirree," Willie said.

The boys started at a soft laugh and turned to see Two-Horse watching them. They turned away quickly and began twisting the auger into the wood. "He gives me the jim-jams," Willie whispered.

"Hush," Eddie said. "He can hear your heart beat. All those Injuns can."

When they'd sunk the first hole eight inches into the beam, they went to the other end and drilled a second hole. Uncle Mac came out of the shop with two long bolts and measured their ends against the width of the holes. "The bolts will have to support a lot of weight," he said, "but these should do."

"Are we going to move it inside tonight?" Jeremy asked.

"No. I want to cut it down a little more first." He centered one of the bolts and, with a grunt, started driving it into the beam with the short-handled sledgehammer.

Once he had the bolts started, he let the boys drive them home. He paid each of the twins a nickel. They accepted, bobbing their heads and scurrying off. "How did they talk you into letting them have a drink of beer?" he asked.

Jeremy took a breath and confessed. "They said they'd tell Mr. Weister what we heard when we hid below the window yesterday. About how Nancy Two-Horse is going to model for the statue." He looked down, feeling his face redden.

"I thought I heard some rustling out there."

"I'm sorry, Uncle Mac. We shouldn't have listened."

"Well, I can understand how you'd be curious. But next time I send you for beer, don't let them have a drink no matter what they threaten. There are already enough problems with drinking in that home."

"I don't think they'll tell now. I think you scared them."

Uncle Mac nodded. "Well, come. Let's rouse Brother Murphy and get some supper."

Jeremy was about to ask if they should invite Two-Horse, but when he looked at the old Indian's spot behind the shop, it was empty except for the long shadow of the maple tilting toward the river in the falling light.

Chapter 7

☽

The next morning Jeremy followed Uncle Mac down the dim stairs into the basement of Callahan's. "What are we looking for?" he asked.

"The old changing screen that used to be upstairs. Your father said it's down here somewhere."

"Oh, I know where that is," Jeremy said, remembering the tall screen with the folding panels that had stood in the corner of his parents' bedroom when his mother was alive. "It's behind some empty crates in the far room. What do we need that for?"

"To keep prying eyes from seeing what we're doing in the shop."

They pushed the crates aside and freed the changing screen. A large rat scuttled across the floor and disappeared beneath the door to the coal cellar. "Better find a trap and set it before that rat wanders into the store," Uncle Mac said. "Fitch would throw a fit."

* * *

Uncle Mac set the screen inside the door, unfolding its panels to block the view from the street. "Now we'll be able to keep the door open for air and still have our privacy," he said. "There's a roll of muslin on the workbench. Tack some over the windows. Then even the Cripshank boys won't find a way to peek in."

While Jeremy tacked squares of the coarse white cloth over the windows, Uncle Mac lettered a sign: NO ORDERS UNTIL FURTHER NOTICE. He hung it beside the shop door and then sat down to sharpen the curved blade of an adz. "An adz works best when you can swing it between your legs," he said. "But the beam is too big to straddle, so I'll have to work from the side."

"Can I help?"

Uncle Mac hesitated. "This is a very dangerous tool, Jeremy. Perhaps you'd better watch this time."

The answer didn't surprise Jeremy; he'd heard it in one form or another a thousand times. But that didn't take the sting out of it. Just when would Uncle Mac trust him with something sharper than a tack hammer? For an instant, the resentment blurred his vision so that he missed the head of the tack and struck his thumb instead. He yelped.

Uncle Mac looked up from his sharpening. "Hit your thumb?"

"Just nicked it," Jeremy said through gritted teeth, and was thankful when Uncle Mac didn't deliver his usual advice: "Keep your mind on your work and keep counting your fingers."

The rest of the morning, Uncle Mac cut with the adz to reduce the weight of the beam. Murphy, Sven, and the silent, smiling Soupy came to the shop a few minutes before noon. "Could you use some help moving that beam, Brother Mac?" Murphy asked.

"I could, indeed, Brother Murphy. If you'd lend a hand, I'd be grateful."

Murphy whispered loudly behind his hand to Sven and Soupy, "For a Protestant Scot, he ain't a bad fellow. And his nephew and great nephew wear a good Irish name."

"The drink has fuddled you again, Murph," Sven said. "All laboring men are brothers. None of the rest makes any difference."

"I stand corrected by a heathen Scandahoovian agitator. I accept it. But come on, lads. That beam won't get lighter by us staring at it."

They became serious as they set about moving the beam. Soupy and Sven slid a short, thick pole under the bolt in the end of the beam nearest the door and prepared to lift. Uncle Mac moved to help Murphy, but Murphy waved him away, squatted, and with a grunt, lifted the other end by himself.

Jeremy held the door as the three lumberjacks wrestled the beam into the shop. The room suddenly seemed very small and the beam very large. Uncle Mac hurried to position a sawhorse under Murphy's end. Face streaming with sweat, Murphy lowered it so that the heavy bolt dropped into the notch in the crossbar of the sawhorse.

Jeremy slid a sawhorse under the other end, hesitated, and then said, "It's lined up. Lower away."

Sven and Soupy eased down their end of the beam, the bolt dropping neatly into the slot. Jeremy let out a breath. Soupy smiled at him with snuff-stained teeth and clapped him on the shoulder.

Over on Eau Claire Street, the clock on the courthouse began striking noon. "Murph, we gotta go," Sven said.

Murphy nodded. "We've got a couple days' work north of town. Farmer wants some sticks dropped and bucked so he can haul 'em to a little mill they've got up there. Ain't much of a job, but the big mills don't hire the likes of us 'cause we might talk sense to the other boys. So we have to take what we can get until Westerhaus sends us all west."

Uncle Mac started to reach into his pocket for his coin purse. "Let me—"

Murphy waved a hand. "No need. You paid us well the day we brought the stick up here. The lads and me agreed that this one'd be on the house."

After dinner, Uncle Mac stretched out on the sofa. "Where are you off to this afternoon?" he asked Jeremy.

"I was going to ask Willie and Eddie if they wanted to go fishing, but it looks like rain. So I don't know. I might just stick around the shop. If I wouldn't be in the way, that is."

"No, you're always a help. But I'm going to catch thirty-nine winks before I go back. Nancy Two-Horse is coming about three for me to make some sketches."

"Oh?" Jeremy said, trying to sound only mildly interested, though he'd known all along that she was coming.

Uncle Mac smiled faintly. "She'll be here. Two-Horse, too, I imagine." He closed his eyes.

Jeremy couldn't tell if the smile was at his expense or not. Nor could he remember exactly when in the last few days he'd begun to think all the time about Nancy Two-Horse. None of the girls his age made him feel anything at all. Oh, he liked some of them well enough as friends, but thinking of Nancy—who wasn't really a girl at all, of course, but already a woman—brought an odd feeling, half queasy, half delicious, to his stomach.

He tried to read the *Old Curiosity Shop*, a book Mrs. Higgins had given him for his birthday, but couldn't concentrate on the story of Little Nell. He looked into the parlor to see if Uncle Mac had exhausted his "thirty-nine winks" (the fortieth being for lazy people only). But the old man still slept, his sparse white hair disarranged on the sofa arm and his big, callused hands folded placidly on his stomach.

Jeremy crossed the street under a gray sky drooping with rain clouds. Inside, the shop was dim, and he busied himself with pumping and lighting the Coleman lamps that hung on opposite walls. He lit and rehung the first of the lamps, stepping off the stool as the light spread with the brightening of the twin gas mantles. He jumped back then, because Two-Horse was squatting in the corner beyond the cold stove, his black eyes glinting in the light.

Two-Horse spoke softly. "What, boy? Do you think I can appear and disappear?" Jeremy stood shaking, unable to answer, and Two-Horse chuckled. "It's not magic, boy. Only stillness."

"I . . . I'm sorry," Jeremy said.

Two-Horse cocked his head quizzically. "Why are you sorry? I am beyond caring if white people see me or not."

Jeremy did not know how to reply and his question surprised him. "Can you show me how?"

"To be still?"

Jeremy nodded.

Two-Horse smiled. "Not as still as an Anishinaabe. What you call a Chippewa. But perhaps more still than most noisy little white boys. Come." He patted the floor beside him. "Squat like I do." Jeremy did. "Now empty your mind and listen." He began chanting softly.

"What does it mean?" Jeremy asked.

"Nothing you have to know. Listen, and when I stop, keep listening."

Jeremy did, and when Two-Horse stopped singing, he hardly noticed, because the song went on in his head until after what seemed like both a long time and no time at all, he became aware of the ache in his thighs and had to put a knee down on the floor. He glanced at Two-Horse, who squatted in a stillness so complete that he seemed almost a statue except for the glitter of his eyes behind their half-closed lids.

They heard a soft footfall on the far side of the screen. Two-Horse spoke in Chippewa, and Nancy stepped around it. "The boy is learning stillness," Two-Horse said. "Or as much of it as a white boy can learn."

Nancy gazed at Jeremy, and Jeremy felt his cheeks redden. "He should first see what his friends are doing. The noisy ones who listened with him beneath the window when we spoke with McAlester."

Jeremy stood, his cheeks so hot that he was sure they glowed. "Uh, where are they?"

"Outside making a peeking hole." She set a bundle down on a bench. "If I catch them trying to peek while I'm changing my clothes, I'll throw them in the river. Tell them that."

"Yes, ma'am."

"Go chase them away and then fetch McAlester. I'll be changed by the time you get back."

Near the corner of the rear wall, Jeremy found the spot where Willie and Eddie had dug out a small knot and tried to expand the hole so that they could see everything going on inside the shop. He looked around angrily and then shouted their names. The twins emerged sheepishly from behind the fence.

Jeremy pointed at the hole. "What did you think you were doing?"

Eddie shrugged. "Just trying to find out what's going on. We saw the screen your uncle put up. And that's not fair. I mean, we helped guard the log and we helped move it and we helped cut it and drill the holes. We got a right to see what he's doing with it."

"Yeah," said Willie. "What's the big deal, anyway? It's just going to be a stupid statue of an Injun girl."

"Hush!" Jeremy glanced around quickly. "You're not supposed to tell."

"Who cares?" Willie said.

"Nobody we know," Eddie said.

"Well, I do. And so does Uncle Mac. So don't get us mad, or we'll tell about you guys sneaking beer all the time. So help me, we will."

The twins shuffled. "Well, you got to tell us what's going on then," Eddie said. "Maybe even give us a peek now and then."

"Okay, if you promise not to tell. Really, really promise."

"We promise," said Eddie.

"Really, really," said Willie.

"Not even if Weister offers you a hundred bucks?"

They nodded.

"Okay," Jeremy said. "Get this hole filled in while I get Uncle Mac up from his nap."

Two-Horse adjusted Nancy's headband of beads and stood back to study her. Then he nodded and returned to his corner.

Uncle Mac handed Jeremy a notepad. "Write down what I tell you. I'm going to take some measurements." He took a cloth tape measure from a pocket and hesitated. "That's if it's all right with you, Nancy."

Nancy tossed back her long braid and extended an arm without speaking. Uncle Mac measured from shoulder to elbow, elbow to wrist, and wrist to fingertips. Jeremy wrote the figures down, trying to steady the slight quiver in his fingers.

Uncle Mac made measurements for twenty minutes, then asked Nancy to stand on a stool so that he could sketch her. She did what he asked, but became quickly bored, shifting and fidgeting on the stool until Two-Horse spoke sharply to her in Chippewa.

After that she seemed to remember something of stillness. Her chin came up, her limbs quieted, and her eyes took on a far-off look. Whether it was a look of listening or remembering, Jeremy couldn't tell. Not that it mattered; watching her was enough for him at the moment, even though the odd feeling he had in the pit of his stomach made no more sense to him now than it had before.

For two hours Uncle Mac circled Nancy, making sketches from different angles. Outside, it began raining, first heavy drops and then a steady spring rain. Jeremy pumped up the lamps so that the mantles glowed bright, chasing the gloom into the far corners.

Finally Uncle Mac seemed to become aware of the passage of time. "Thank you, Nancy," he said.

"You are welcome," she said primly, stepped down, and went to the chair where she'd folded her city clothes. Jeremy felt himself blush at the thought of her changing.

"Come on, Jeremy," Uncle Mac said. "We'll go across to the store and drink a soda."

As he followed, Jeremy felt a draft of rainy air and heard the soft closing of the rear door of the shop. He glanced into Two-Horse's corner and found it empty.

Chapter 8

☽

Nancy Two-Horse came twice more in the next three days, and both times Jeremy felt his insides twist with unaccountable feelings. He had heard, of course, about the love between men and women; had even heard the word *infatuation* and knew that it held a less honorable, even a laughable place on the list of human emotions. He had never, however, imagined himself the helpless victim of love or infatuation. When it came his time to court, he would be coolly sophisticated, accepting the adoration of beautiful, laughing, fair-skinned girls as his due. And his coolness would, of course, further inflame their passion for him, making deep feeling on his part neither necessary nor desirable.

But Nancy resembled none of his imaginings. She was dark, not fair. He had never heard her laugh or even seen her truly smile. And, most fantastic of all, she was five, perhaps six years older than he was. Yet his heart leaped with each sight, each thought of her.

* * *

At breakfast on the morning after Nancy's third visit, Uncle Mac said, "You can be with your friends today. You haven't had much time with them lately."

Jeremy looked at him in surprise. "Don't you need me?"

"No, I need some time to think and sketch. Two-Horse has gone home to tend his garden, and I told Nancy that I wouldn't need her for a few days."

Jeremy felt more relief than loss at the prospect of not seeing Nancy. He was sure that he had hidden his infatuation from Uncle Mac, and he was almost certain that Nancy, too, had no hint of his fevered state. Now, for a few days, he might once again be as free as the Cripshank twins. He must, of course, be careful not to hint to them of what he felt for Nancy. Eddie would be quick to point out every impossibility for such a love, while Willie would announce, with all the assurance of the truly stupid, the greatest flaw: Nancy was an Indian with all the inferiorities of her race to the likes of the Cripshanks and theirs.

Jeremy left the apartment by the back stairs to avoid Mr. Fitch, who had a habit of sending him on errands whenever Mr. Callahan's absence gave him the chance to order his employer's son about. So intent was he on closing the back door without making a sound that he didn't spot Eddie and Willie sitting in the front seat of Dr. Curtis's new Reo touring car. "Hey, you snubbing us or you gone deaf?" Eddie called.

"Come on, hop in," Willie said. "We're goin' to Chicago." Jeremy took a quick look up and down the alley and then hurried to the automobile. He was about to ask if he could sit in the driver's seat when Arlyn came to the back door of

Callahan's to shake a rug. "Hey, you boys, get out of there! Jeremy, you know better than that."

"I ain't done anything."

"But you were about to. Now get going before Dr. Curtis catches you."

For an hour the boys wandered the streets of downtown, finding nothing to equal the brief joy provided by the Reo. They crossed over the Barstow Street Bridge to the North Side, pausing to spit into the waters of the Eau Claire. They followed the smaller river down to where it joined the Chippewa, then wandered up the shore to the foot of the railroad bridge across the big river. "Let's go back over to the West Side," Eddie said. "Gotta be more going on over there."

"River's down," Willie said. "Maybe we'll find something on the beach worth hocking."

It wasn't much of a hope, Jeremy knew, but it sounded as good a plan as any. Still, he hesitated. "We're not going to cross here, are we?"

"Why not?" Eddie asked. "You gone yellow or something?"

"No, but after that kid got killed over in Menomonie last fall, Pa made me promise never to cross on the railroad bridge."

"So what? That kid in Menomonie was stupid, and your pa's out of town."

The twins started out onto the tarred timbers, but Jeremy hung back. "Come on, chicken liver," Willie yelled.

"I ain't chicken-livered," Jeremy said, "but I ain't stupid, either. I'm going down over Grand Avenue."

The twins made chicken sounds, but Jeremy ignored them. He hurried toward Barstow, glancing back a couple of times to watch the twins sauntering across the railroad bridge. He half hoped that a train would come, not so fast as to really put them in danger but fast enough to make them run.

On the south side of the Eau Claire, he cut off Barstow onto River Street, dodging along the busy sidewalks until he reached Grand Avenue. He was halfway across the bridge when he spotted Agnes, Willie and Eddie's older sister, striding grimly toward him. Agnes was someone to avoid. At seventeen, she was a bulky, homely girl with a quick temper and a hard hand. The twins feared her and so did Jeremy. But it was too late to flee.

"Where are those two?" she snapped. Jeremy fumbled for an answer, and one of Agnes's big hands shot out to grab a fistful of his shirt. "Don't try any lies on me, you little brat!"

"They're over there." He pointed to the west side of the river. "They crossed on the railroad bridge."

She squinted upstream, spotted the two small figures, and let go his shirt. "Come on. We gotta go get 'em."

Jeremy hurried to keep up. "What's the matter?"

"Accident at the mill. Pa got his hand caught in one of the belts. Tore off half his fingers."

"Jeez. I'm sorry, Agnes."

"Yeah, me, too. He weren't worth much before, he ain't gonna be worth horse dung now. All comes down to Agnes having to work harder. Agnes having to do more. Agnes having to go out and get another job." She glared at him. "You know how long I been workin'?"

"Uh, no."

"Ask me how long."

"How long?"

"Since I was nine years old, that's how long. Did I get to go to school and sit around learnin' letters and numbers and all that stuff? Uh-uh, not Agnes. Agnes was too stupid. Agnes had to go to work so her little brothers and sisters could go to school. Well, it ain't made Willie smart yet, and it ain't made Eddie smart enough to keep his mouth shut when he oughta. Now things is gonna change. Some others gonna have to start pulling some of the load now that Pa's crippled up."

Jeremy hesitated, because it was never wise to ask Agnes anything without thinking first. "How's your ma doing?"

Agnes snorted. "Lyin' across her bed, bawlin' like a baby. She knows we're caught in the wringer now. The whole lot of us, just like a bunch of darned ol' wet towels." She seemed pleased with this image and smiled grimly.

As they reached the far side of the bridge, Willie glanced up from the gravel beach and spotted them. He froze. Before he could recover, Agnes screamed at him: "Don't you dare run, Willie Cripshank! I'll chase you down and thrash you like you ain't never been thrashed before."

The twins hung their heads and waited for whatever punishment Agnes was about to hand out. Jeremy trailed along behind while Agnes snarled the news of the accident at them and her own determination not to be the only martyred one in the Cripshank household. Willie asked questions, more in wonder at the how of the accident than curiosity at the extent of the injury. Jeremy saw that Eddie had gone stiff, perhaps because he'd already guessed answers to questions that Willie wouldn't think to ask for a long time.

Jeremy parted from them with a mumbled condolence at the corner of Niagara and Third Avenue. He walked home the long way, across the Water Street Bridge and through the Third Ward. Here, in a few blocks along the east side of the Chippewa, stood the great mansions of the lumber barons. The children of these homes wore frocks and sailor suits, rode in automobiles and carriages, and studied with tutors or at boarding schools. When the log drives came downstream, they rushed not to the riverbank but to windows and balconies high above the Chippewa. And though Jeremy could only guess at what went on in the minds and hearts of such children, he knew somehow that nothing could ever really touch them, that whatever hardships they were to know in life would be in no way like Willie's and Eddie's, or even his own.

Uncle Mac unlocked the shop door and led the way to the pine beam. "Come have a look at the maiden," he said.

Jeremy stared. Usually, Uncle Mac made only a few pencil marks to block out the eventual shape of whatever he was going to carve. But this time he'd sketched the entire figure on the wood in broad chalk strokes, even shading the tucks and folds of the maiden's doeskin dress and the tapering and turns of her legs, arms, and neck. Only her face was eerily featureless, like a gibbous moon through frosted glass.

"She doesn't have a face," Jeremy said.

"No, not yet. Were you eavesdropping when Two-Horse told me I couldn't use Nancy's face?"

"Yes. But I thought you'd get around that. Make her face a little narrower or her mouth a little wider, but that it'd still be her. I mean, she's so beautiful, Uncle Mac. How can you do better?"

Uncle Mac raised his eyebrows. "She's pretty. I'm not sure I'd call her beautiful."

Jeremy felt his cheeks warm. "I meant pretty."

Uncle Mac nodded. "Well, we'll just have to see if Two-Horse is right about another face coming to us. For now, let's see if we can do something with the rest of her."

All through that day Uncle Mac worked with a hatchet, the blows almost as regular as the metronome Professor Hauenstein sometimes used during Jeremy's piano lessons. Jeremy swept up the white, fragrant chips and dumped them in the kindling box beside the barrel stove. "You're going to have a lot of tinder for the fall," he said. Uncle Mac only grunted, his eyes and hands intent on the work.

When Two-Horse came into the shop in the early afternoon, Uncle Mac stepped back to show him the work. Two-Horse studied it without expression, then nodded and walked past Jeremy to his corner, where he squatted and fell into stillness.

Uncle Mac worked for two days with the hatchet, then set it aside and rechalked the outline of the figure. On the morning of the third day, he started working with a wooden mallet and a large chisel.

The next afternoon Nancy came to the shop and stood looking at the figure for a long time before stepping onto the stool so that Uncle Mac could take more measurements. She paid no notice to Jeremy, though he stood as close to her as he dared. Only after Uncle Mac had finished taking the measurements and making another rapid sketch did she turn to gaze at Jeremy, her dark eyes searching his.

Jeremy found Eddie and Willie sitting on a driftwood log left behind on the beach by the great flood three years before. Willie slouched loose-jointed, whittling a stick with his barlow knife, but Eddie sat stiffly, arms hugged to his chest, as if chilled despite the warmth of the evening. For a moment Jeremy found himself hesitant. "Hey, guys, where you been hiding?"

Willie looked up and grinned. "Been lookin' for work. Need to help out more now that Pa got himself tore up."

"How is he?"

Willie shrugged. "Ain't seen him since the day they let him out of the hospital. He weren't doing too bad then, considering."

"Meaning he was drunk," Eddie snapped. "Didn't even come home. Just took the money the men at work tossed into the hat and went down to O'Sullivan's to get drunk."

For a long moment, no one spoke. Willie started whittling again, whistling softly through his teeth. "So, what kind of work did you find?" Jeremy asked.

"We start at Valley One tomorrow," Eddie said.

"Stacking lumber for a few days? If Pa'd let me, I'd—"

"No, inside. Permanent-like."

"But you can't! You're not old enough to work on the saws. My pa says there are laws about that stuff now."

"Your pa!" Eddie turned blazing eyes on him. "Don't go telling me what your pa says. Because he's like all the others who say things have changed. But things never change for us. Ain't nobody gonna go down to Valley One and tell the boss that Willie and Eddie Cripshank ain't old enough to work in the mill, that we oughta be out havin' fun, maybe sellin' a couple of newspapers or stacking a little lumber, till it's time to go back to school, where we can learn to be doctors or lawyers or teachers. People like us never get to be doctors or lawyers or teachers. We go to work in the mills and get our fingers tore off, then get drunk and get tossed out of our homes. Nobody gives a holler about the likes of us, Jeremy. Nobody!"

Jeremy had taken a step backward. He turned helplessly to Willie. "Willie, tell him."

Willie laughed. "Tell him what? Hey, I'm ready. I don't wanta go back to school. Agnes is right, I'm too stupid to learn anything. I'm okay with the mill. Eddie, he's just mad because he wanted to be a t—"

"You shut up, Willie!" Eddie snapped.

Willie smiled, shrugged, and mouthed "teacher" to Jeremy. He draped an arm around his brother's shoulders. "Hey, come on, Eddie. Ain't gonna be so bad."

"What time do you start?" Jeremy asked.

"Told us to come in at eight in the morning," Willie said. "By that time the shift'll be goin' strong and they can work us in. After that it's six to six, exceptin' Sunday. Three weeks on days, then three weeks on nights."

69

"Maybe if I talked to my pa. He'll be back by the end of next week. Maybe he—"

"Don't!" Eddie snapped. "You'll just mess things up."

Willie grinned at Jeremy. "Hey, it's the best money around. We'll be okay. You'll see."

Chapter 9

☽

Eddie came down the creaking porch steps, carrying his lunch in a burlap sack. Jeremy lifted a hand. "Hey, Eddie."

"You gonna try talking us out of this?"

"No, just thought I'd walk with you."

"It ain't no disgrace what we're doing, you know."

"I know."

Willie came out, turning at the door to call, "See you later, Ma. We'll be home hungry." He bounced down the steps. "Hey, Jeremy. Gonna give the mill a try? It'll beat school."

"Nah, I'm gonna stick with the books for a while."

"Well, read one for me. I sure ain't gonna bother."

They set off after Eddie, who was marching grimly down the street. "Does Eddie really want to be a teacher?" Jeremy asked.

"Sometimes. Other times it's other things. But he likes school, so this is hard for him."

"Murphy says that if the mill had a union, then injured men would—"

Willie held up a hand. "Don't even tell me. This is my first day and I ain't gonna start worrying about no unions."

"Well, sometime you ought to listen to him."

"Uh-uh. I figure the guy who owns the mill knows how to run his business better than me."

They caught up to Eddie and turned down Fifth Avenue toward the river. Rounding the corner onto Water Street, they met Hans Weister. "Boys! How are you?" He reached out great, meaty hands to take the twins by the shoulders. "I was sorry to hear about your father's accident. How is he?"

Eddie tried to shrug from under the weight of Weister's hand. "He's okay, Mr. Weister. Excuse us, but we gotta hurry 'fore we're late to work."

Weister lifted pale eyebrows. "Work, is it? At Valley One?"

"Yes, sir."

"Well, you're a couple of solid-looking boys. I think you'll do just fine." He dug in a pocket and produced a pair of quarters. "But don't forget your old friend, Hans Weister. You hear anything down at the mill that might be useful to a businessman like me, you come tell me."

The twins took the coins, and though Jeremy wished otherwise, he knew that he might well have done the same. "Hey, thanks, Mr. Weister," Willie said.

"Yeah, thanks," Eddie mumbled.

"My pleasure," Weister said. He looked over their heads at Jeremy. "And you, young Jeremy, can always bring me a story or two from that store of your pa's. No harm in it. I'm just a curious man who likes to hear things and help people." He slapped the twins' shoulders and sauntered down the sidewalk.

The boys had grown up hearing the whine of the great band saws cutting lumber in the mills along the Chippewa. It was not a sound they noticed often, and when they passed one of the mills, they unconsciously raised their voices to be heard. But this day, as they came under the shadow of the three tall stacks of Valley One, the sound of the saws became a real thing again—a protesting scream each time a carriage-strapped log rammed forward into the teeth of a saw.

Jeremy hesitated at the gate, but then followed the twins, unwilling to abandon them yet. A blast of hot air struck them at the foot of the tall doors. In the half darkness within, machines roared and men shouted. Plumes of vapor hissed from steam lines, and the floor itself seemed to bulge with the heat of the boilers below.

Twenty feet from them, a broad plank fell away from a pine log dogged atop a carriage. In his splinter cage, the sawyer pulled a lever to bring the log back from the saw. He gauged the next cut, raising a hand to signal the setter riding the carriage, and then threw the lever forward. The log lunged back into the band saw. Steel teeth, running in a continuous belt faster than the eye could follow, sliced into the wood with a shriek that made the boys throw their hands over their ears.

A figure loomed up in front of them—a man, huge and dark, his bare arms and shoulders glistening with sweat. "You Cripshank's boys?" he shouted. Willie and Eddie bobbed their heads. "Didn't know there was three of ya. Well, no matter. Come on. You'll be feedin' slab wood to the boiler." He pushed the twins in front of him and then turned to stare at Jeremy. "Well, come on, boy."

"I'm . . . I'm not one of them," Jeremy hollered. "I . . . I just came along to see them get started."

"Well, you seen it. Now off with ya. Come back when you're ready to do a man's work."

Jeremy backed away, watching as the foreman pushed Willie and Eddie toward the dark stairs leading down to the boiler room. Then he turned and ran, almost blindly, toward the gate and the sunlit street.

For a few days Jeremy found refuge in the quiet of the shop, where one old man chiseled away at the statue and the other watched silently from the shadows of his corner. The maiden lay between the sawhorses, attached head and foot to blocks of uncarved beam but fully formed in limb and torso. Uncle Mac had carved the head so that her face was no longer the moon shape of the chalk outline on wood, yet Jeremy found the lack of features disquieting. If Nancy had no objection, why not model the maiden's face after hers? But when he tried to question Uncle Mac one morning before Two-Horse arrived, the old man shook his head. "In Two-Horse's belief, it would do Nancy harm. And I have given my word. Hand me a smaller chisel, please."

Jeremy had become expert at sharpening and took pride that Uncle Mac could never ask for a chisel that wouldn't have a razor edge. Beyond that, he had little to do but fetch and sweep. He tried now and then to practice some of the stillness Two-Horse had taught him, but with small success since the outdoors of sunlight and street noise always called to him.

The noon whistle brought release after the long mornings. Mrs. Higgins chastised him for bolting his food, but he ate hurriedly to lose as little of the afternoons as possible. On the streets of downtown, he found friends. They played baseball in the park at the foot of Gilbert Avenue, sold papers on the street corners, and nagged Lester for a chance to curry and feed the horses at the livery stable. Bored with the town, they climbed to the top of the bluff along the East Side, where the houses thinned and orchards still grew around the cemetery overlooking the rivers. Jeremy's mother was buried there, in a shady place beneath the overhanging boughs of a cedar. But he did not tell these boys so, nor did he go to find her grave, though he remembered where she lay more clearly than he remembered anything about her.

When he swept the shop in the late afternoons, the pine shavings tumbled golden in the light from the window high under the peak of the roof. The warm, clean odor of pine floated around him, and he found himself not unhappy with the promise of the quiet evening before him. After his chores, he would eat supper and then fish in solitude for an hour along the edge of the diminishing pack of logs.

Yet, in those moments by the river, he could not help but see the tall stacks of Valley One. And then, though he knew of no good reason, he felt like a coward.

✳ ✳ ✳

Iris shook her head, and Jeremy relaxed the reins to let her nibble at the dewy grass growing in the cracks of the brick sidewalk by the train station. He had wanted to talk more to his father on the weekend, but Mr. Callahan had arrived home exhausted and done little but sleep and eat for two days. Now it was Monday morning and again they waited for the train.

"I'm sorry, son," Mr. Callahan said. "But the opportunity we have in La Crosse just won't wait. It's not often that a competitor goes bust without anyone guessing beforehand. If I can pick up most of Beard & Lowe's wholesale customers, Callahan's will be a very successful business. I might even be able to afford a fancy eastern college for you in a few years. Would you like that?"

"Sure, Pa. But, Pa, if you do get Beard & Lowe's customers, do you think there'll be enough work for you to hire Willie and Eddie for the warehouse?"

Mr. Callahan grimaced. "I'm sorry, Jeremy, but we wouldn't expand the warehouse here. We'll use Beard & Lowe's in La Crosse and keep on as many of their people as we can."

"But it isn't fair what's happened to Willie and Eddie! Willie doesn't mind so much, but Eddie wanted to be a teacher."

"I never guessed that."

"Neither did I, but Willie told me. That's why Eddie feels so bad about leaving school."

"I'm sorry, son. There's nothing I can afford to do."

"But, Pa, it's not fair!"

"No, it's not. Sometimes it doesn't seem like much of life is. They're not bad boys. I like them both. But I never thought they'd have any other kind of life. They were bound from the start to end up in one of the mills. And when the logs are all gone and the sawmills close, they'll go to work in a mill of some other kind."

"And there's no hope for anything else?" Jeremy asked bitterly.

"Not now. That's why I think your friend Murphy has a lot that people ought to hear. And I say that even though I don't always agree with the methods unions use. Especially his IWW."

Jeremy stared. "Murphy's a Wobbly?"

Mr. Callahan chuckled. "Sure he is. Did you expect him to have horns? They're just men. Angry men sometimes, but just men."

"I guess I just thought that all the Wobblies were somewhere else."

"Nope. Some are right here." Up the track, a whistle blew. "Well, we can talk more when I get back next week. I'm sorry about Willie and Eddie, son. I'd do something if I could."

"Pa, why do I feel so bad? Why do I feel like a coward for not going with them?"

Mr. Callahan chewed his lip for a moment. "For lack of any better word, I guess I'd call it friendship."

Every day for the next three days Jeremy crossed the bridge to the West Side and waited at the entrance to Valley One for Willie and Eddie to come off shift. He wasn't quite sure why, since the twins were too tired to play or even to talk much. But he walked home with them, embarrassed by his clean clothes.

On Thursday, Murphy and Sven were standing near the gate, talking to a couple of mill hands waiting to go on shift. Murphy held out a leaflet to one of them. "Just read it, brother. Ain't gonna hurt you none. Tells you all about the Brothers in Labor and the Industrial Workers of the World."

The man shook his head. "I can't, friend. Ain't that I'm against the IWW. More power to you boys, I say. But them that runs Valley don't hold with none of that bummery. Catch me with some Wobbly paper and I'd lose my job. And I got a wife and eight young'uns to feed. I need my pay."

"We all do, brother. But how much are they paying you in there, just so you can ruin your health to make a bunch of rich men richer? How much time they give you to spend with your family? I'll bet some of your little ones hardly know who you are."

The man laughed. "True. But I still can't help you, friend." He passed through the gate. The other man followed, seeming to ignore the pamphlet Sven offered him. But at the last second he snatched it, shoving it out of sight in a pocket of his overalls.

Murphy leaned back against the fence. "What are they so afraid of, Brother Sven?"

Sven spat. "Company goons, same as always."

Murphy saw Jeremy. "Well, hello, lad. Come down to learn more about the Brothers in Labor?" He held out a pamphlet.

Jeremy hesitated, then told himself not to be a coward and took it. "Thanks. I'll read it when I get home."

"Good lad. And how have you been?"

"Pretty good. Where's Soupy?"

"Went down to Durand to see his wife. Hadn't gotten around to seeing her since last summer and figured he'd better before Westerhaus sends the train to take us all west."

"I never knew he had a wife. He got kids?"

"A boy who went off someplace and a girl who ain't quite right in the head. Daughter and the wife got a little farm. Just a cow, a few chickens, a hog or two, and a big garden. But it gets 'em by."

The whistle blew and Murphy straightened. "Well, time to work on these boyos. Try to make 'em see the light of the brotherhood of all workers."

Jeremy crossed the street to avoid the stream of mill hands pushing through the gate. Perhaps because they were small and easily swept along, Willie and Eddie emerged ahead of most of the off-coming shift. They came out sooty and so tired they stumbled. Eddie tried to say something to Jeremy, but his voice cracked dryly. He shook his head and trudged up the street toward home.

Willie smiled tiredly. "I keep tellin' him it's gonna get better. We just ain't used to it yet. Don't worry. I'm helpin' him along."

After all the years they'd called Willie stupid and played tricks on him, it was odd to hear him acting the strong, grown-up one. "I hope it gets easier soon."

"It will. We ain't the first to start in the boiler room. And Maddox, the foreman, he ain't so bad. He's hard, but he don't let no one bully us."

At the corner of Fifth and Niagara, Willie paused. "Hey, Jeremy, I 'preciate you coming down here. But it's hard on Eddie. Gets him thinking how things might be different. So maybe you oughta stay away for a while. Not, you know, forever. We're gonna have some good times again, but it's hard on him now. You understand, don't you?"

Jeremy bit his lip. "Yeah, sure."

Willie slapped him on the shoulder and walked up Niagara toward home. Jeremy felt tears come to his eyes and furiously blinked them away.

He walked, head down, back toward Water Street. He was almost there when he heard shouts and curses. He ran to the corner. Across the street, a knot of men swirled in the midst of the incoming river of workers. Jeremy saw Murphy, blood streaming from a wound in his temple, his face ferocious as he swung an ax handle. He tore one man from a pile, then another, hurling them aside. Sven exploded upward from the tangle, both fists swinging. Back to back, the two men fought their attackers. Murphy clouted one charging man between the eyes, grabbed him by the shirtfront, and raised the ax handle to brain him.

"Here now!" a voice boomed, and Maddox, the giant foreman, waded into the fight. He held out a thick arm to ward off the blow about to fall on the helpless man. A silence fell so complete that Jeremy could hear Murphy's harsh breathing. "Don't do it, Murphy," Maddox growled.

"You'll kill him, and we don't need that. What we got here's bad enough already."

"Then call off your goons."

"They ain't mine, Murphy. I'm a workin' man, same as you."

Murphy spat blood. "You was. But you sold out when you took foreman, Maddox."

"That may be how you see it, but I got no wish to fight you. But you hit that man, and you and me, we're gonna have to do it. That's the way it is, and you know it. So let him go. He ain't worth killing. He ain't even worth hittin' again. Then you and Sven can go your way without any more trouble. My word on it."

Slowly, Murphy lowered the ax handle. He smiled through bloodied lips. "You and me. That would be a fight now, wouldn't it?"

"That it would. Exceptin' I don't have the heart for it. Too much I remember."

Murphy chuckled. "Yes, you and me was a pair once."

"We were that. There are places that'll never forget us."

"What happened?"

"The world changed. We cut the pine. We got older."

Murphy nodded. He looked down at the dazed man he held by the shirtfront as if he'd just now remembered him. He spoke over his shoulder. "Brother Sven, are you ready to quit these inhospitable surroundings?"

"For the moment, Brother Murphy, but I intend to return."

"As do I." He opened his fist, and the dazed man sagged into Maddox's arms.

Maddox looked at him in disgust, then shoved him toward two of his companions. "All right, part the way. These men are leaving, and anyone who gives them any trouble answers to me." He stared balefully at Murphy and Sven. "Now I'd be obliged if you did the leaving."

Murphy grinned. "You smiled more in the old days, Aaron."

"There was a powerful lot more to smile at, Colin."

For a moment longer, they stood facing each other, aloof from all the smaller men around them, then Murphy nodded and led Sven through the crowd.

Chapter 10

☽

Jeremy was sweeping the sidewalk in front of McAlester's Woodcarving when Murphy came up the street. His lips were swollen and his face was purple with bruises, yet the big man walked jauntily. He grinned at Jeremy, showing a newly chipped tooth. "And how did you like the donnybrook fair, lad?"

"You would have whupped 'em if that big foreman hadn't stopped you."

Murphy laughed. "I fear not, lad. They had us pretty well outnumbered. I was glad to see old Maddox, even if he has gone company." He gestured toward the door. "Is your uncle in?"

"Yes. But give me a second to see if he wants to cover the maiden. He's gotten kinda funny about that recently."

"Oh ho." Murphy laughed. "What? Doesn't she have any clothes on?"

Jeremy felt a sudden irritation. "She's got clothes! They're not painted yet, but it ain't like she's naked."

Murphy grinned. "Easy, lad. You're swelled up like a banty rooster protecting his lady's virtue."

Jeremy had a sudden image of how he must appear in the big man's eyes. He clamped his mouth shut, trying to hide his embarrassment, but then had to laugh. "No, it's nothing about her clothes at all. But now that he's started carving her face, he doesn't want anyone to see her until he's finished."

Uncle Mac called from inside the shop. "Let him in, Jeremy. I want to see what the company's finest did to Brother Murphy."

They stepped into the coolness of the shop. Murphy bowed to Uncle Mac and Two-Horse. "And how fare you men today? I would call you gentlemen, except that I think too highly of you."

Uncle Mac's lips twitched into a smile. "You live a hard life, Brother Murphy, and you are even harder on those who would lead easier ones. Just the other night Jeremy's father was talking of sending him east to college in a few years, where he can learn to be one of those gentlemen you despise."

Murphy looked down at Jeremy. "Is that the truth? Well, our lad will be a different sort of gentleman from those who exploit the workers and send their goons to dent good Irish heads. Our lad won't forget his friends who dream of a better world. And perhaps he will do something to make it come to be." He looked at Uncle Mac. "Might there be a cup of blackjack left in the pot?"

"Not hot, I'm afraid. But Mrs. Higgins will have a pot on across the street."

Jeremy said, "I'll get it, Uncle Mac."

When he returned a few minutes later with the steaming coffeepot, Murphy was seated on a stool while Two-Horse examined his injuries. Two-Horse tut-tutted and dipped a rag in a basin. Murphy winced when Two-Horse touched the cloth to a gash at his hairline. "Stupid Irish should have done this yesterday after the fight," Two-Horse grumbled.

"Septic?" Uncle Mac asked.

Two-Horse nodded. "Here also." He pointed to a cut on Murphy's ear. "What did you use to wash it, Irish?"

"Sven and me used a pint of decent whiskey. Ouch! Take it easy, Big Thunder."

Two-Horse snorted. "Whiskey don't work from the inside out, Irish." He turned to Jeremy. "Go ask your dark friend for some of his horse medicine. Strong is best."

"We could take him to young Dr. Curtis," Uncle Mac said.

"Horse medicine's better for a thick-headed Irish, I think," Two-Horse said. He washed the ear again, and Murphy whined.

Jeremy ran down to the livery stable, wondering how Murphy could take and deliver great blows without a wince and then whine like a child when the old Indian cleaned a cut.

Lester sat in a patch of sunlight by the door, polishing the silver medallions on the fancy harness reserved for weddings, funerals, and the Fourth of July parade. "Morning, Jeremy. Come for the big carriage or just to pester your friend Lester?"

"Neither one." Jeremy explained.

Lester frowned. "I wouldn't let Two-Horse doctor me none. Can't tell from one day to the next how he's feeling about white folks."

"Uh, maybe you ain't noticed recently, but you're not exactly white, Lester."

Lester peered into the bright surface of one of the medallions. "Dang! You're right. When'd that happen?"

"Come on, Lester. Can I have the medicine?"

Lester chuckled. "Sure. Just give me a minute and I'll come with you."

Lester got a couple of brown bottles and some bandages, told Rick, the stable boy, that he was going uptown, and then followed Jeremy to the street. "So you saw the fight, did you?"

"Just the last couple of minutes before that big foreman stopped it."

"Maddox's a hard man, but he's straight. He would step in if he saw it wasn't a fair fight. . . . Did you hear the big train's coming? The one that's going to take the logging gangs out west?"

"No. When'd you hear?"

"This morning when I was up waiting for the mail train."

"When's it coming?"

"End of the week. Pickin' up anyone who's interested in going. Except they'll never let Murphy or Sven or any of their Wobbly friends on board."

In the shop Lester joined Two-Horse, and together they doctored Murphy's wounds. After some discussion, none of which included Murphy, they decided to stitch the gash in his forehead. Uncle Mac stepped in with needle and thread. Murphy yelped with each stitch, and Lester and Two-Horse chuckled.

"So," Lester said, "I suppose we should check on the Swedish half of this troublesome twosome."

"Tell Murphy about the train first," Jeremy said.

Lester sobered. "The train's laid on, Murphy. Coming at the end of the week out of the Rapids. Making stops two or three places on the way, so there'll be a bunch on board by the time it gets here."

Murphy's face darkened. "What time is it coming?"

"Round two in the afternoon from what I heard."

"I gotta be on that train. Me and Sven and Soupy, unless Soupy's decided it's finally time for him to settle down to farming. We could have half the boys on board talked around to the union by the time we hit the Dakotas."

"They'll have guards on the platform," Uncle Mac said.

"True, but if we could get by 'em and get on board, there wouldn't be nothin' they could do. The boys on the train wouldn't let 'em."

Jeremy, who'd read enough penny thrillers to know a great deal about trains and train robbers, said, "I know a way. Me and Lester, we could get you on, and they'd never be the wiser until it was too late."

He told them his plan, and they turned it round and round until they finally agreed that it was nearly flawless. Lester grinned. "So, Dr. Two-Horse, should we go attend to Brother Sven?"

Two-Horse nodded. "Come, Irish. Take us to the smarter one of you two."

Murphy turned at the door. "I may not see you again, Brother McAlester. I am beholden to you for the stitches and the coffee and the friendship."

Uncle Mac bowed, almost formally. "The pleasure has been mine."

Murphy pointed at the statue of the maiden, hidden beneath the old sheet. "May I see her before I leave?"

Uncle Mac hesitated for only the briefest of moments. "Of course. Stand there where the light is best." He pulled away the sheet.

The maiden lay as if asleep, her face still indistinct beneath the soft, unsanded wood yet emergent already in its beauty. For a long minute, Murphy said nothing. Then he raised his gaze to Uncle Mac, and Jeremy was shocked to see tears in his blue eyes. "She is like a wood fairy," he whispered. "My mother used to tell tales of the fairies and how some of them made their homes in trees. That's why men have to be very careful when they cut the oldest timber, lest some wood fairy drop a great limb to kill the woodsmen and save her home."

"Even here?" Jeremy asked, unsure as always what to believe when men started talking of the unseen.

Murphy looked again at the maiden. "I had not thought so. But perhaps."

Rumor of the train resolved into fact with the posting of handbills announcing that the Lumberjack Express would roll into Eau Claire at two o'clock on Friday afternoon. The announcement invited all HONEST AND INTREPID SAWYERS, AX MEN, LOADERS, TEAMSTERS, AND RIVER MEN TO BOARD

THE LUMBERJACK EXPRESS FOR HIGH ADVENTURE AND HIGH PAY IN THE GREAT WOODS OF THE NEW NORTHWEST. But at the bottom it warned in small but heavy type: RAILROAD DETECTIVES WILL BE ON THE PLATFORM TO PREVENT THE BOARDING OF ANY ELEMENTS DISRUPTIVE TO THE SUCCESS OF THIS GREAT ENTERPRISE.

Jeremy plucked a copy of the handbill from a fence and brought it to Murphy and Sven, where the two lumberjacks sat in the park at the foot of Porter Street. A bench over-looking the river had become their favorite place in the days since the brawl. They did not complain, but Jeremy could tell from the gingerly way they moved that both had taken more punishment than they would admit.

Murphy read the handbill slowly, his lips moving on the more difficult words. He scoffed and handed it to Sven, who put down his length of rope twisted in its fantastic knots. He squinted at the handbill, shading it from the sun-shine with a palm. He read, then smiled bitterly. "Goons," he said. "Big mills, big railroads. They're all the same."

Murphy leaned back, hands behind his head, eyes closed. "So, shall we follow the plan of our little brother Jeremy? Or shall we sit here for the rest of our days, enjoy-ing God's sunshine?"

Sven gestured at the river, its blanket of logs grown thin so that patches of blue water showed through as the logs drifted. "There's no more to do here. This was the last of the big drives. Soon most of the mills will close. Those that are left will never hire union workers. We have failed here. Perhaps we can do better in the New Northwest."

Murphy didn't open his eyes. "We haven't failed, Brother Sven. There are many good union men here now, even if they can't own to it."

"I tried to talk to my friends Willie and Eddie about the union," Jeremy said, "but they wouldn't listen."

Murphy shrugged. "Those who need the union the most are often the hardest to reach. When the mills close and the hard times come, they'll start seeing things our way. Then when the bosses open new factories, there'll be more union men. In time, there'll be too many for the bosses and their goons to break. The workers will have their rights or shut down the factories. This is going to be a union town someday. I promise you that."

Sven sighed. "But I am a man of the woods. I need trees as well as my union. I say we try to get on board the train."

"Yes, I need the trees, too. So, little brother Jeremy, will you still help us?"

"I will," Jeremy said, "if you'll call me 'brother,' not 'little brother.'"

"As you wish, Brother Jeremy. And Brother Lester? He will help?"

"He wants to. He's already sent his best clothes out to the presser."

"Then let's go talk to him."

Yet none of them moved, held for a few minutes longer by the river and the slow drift of the logs on the water. "Murphy," Jeremy asked, "will it be like here? Will you cut everything?"

"Lord, I hope not, lad. I hope we'll have better sense next time."

They heard footsteps and turned to see Soupy, grinning his gap-toothed grin, coming down the grassy slope, duffel bag on his shoulder. "Brother Soupy!" Murphy laughed. "I had about given up hope. Decided you had to see those big red trees, eh?"

Soupy dropped his duffel, winked at Jeremy, and then stepped to Sven and Murphy to inspect their battered faces. They submitted as if by habit. Soupy shook his head. Sven reached out and patted his arm gently. "It's not that bad, Soupy. We gave better than we got."

"By Patrick, we did!" Murphy said. "Exceptin' the kick some boyo gave me in the ribs, I feel all the better for the tussle. And just look at the beautiful stitching our brother McAlester did on this hard Irish head." He swept back his hair to show the cut.

Sven rose. "Enough time wasted. I'm going to get my gear. Better we find a place nearer the station for tonight. Shall I bring yours along, Murph?"

"No, I'll come with you. The more I think on it, the better for our African brother if he isn't seen with us. We'll leave all to Brother Jeremy." He grinned at the boy.

At noon on Friday, Uncle Mac finished his last bite of pie and leaned back. "I wish I could think of a better way to get Murphy and his friends on board that train."

"Nothing's going to happen to Lester and me, Uncle Mac," Jeremy said. "We'll be fine."

"I just worry someone's going to recognize you. Other boys may come to see the lumberjacks off."

"They'll think it's some kind of joke. We only have to fool the railroad detectives, and they won't recognize us."

"Well, I'll be down at the other end of the platform if things go bad."

"I'm going to get dressed," Jeremy said.

Half an hour later Eddie and Willie wouldn't have recognized Jeremy at second or even third glance. He wore the same Sunday clothes that he always wore, but this time he wore them willingly and, because of that, neatly. He'd scrubbed his skin pink and wore his hair slicked back like one of the rich kids from the Third Ward. Uncle Mac stared at him. Then he laughed. "Well, aren't you the dandy!"

Jeremy doffed his hat.

Lester pulled up at the side door of Callahan's in the livery stable's best buggy. His dark Sunday suit was brushed and pressed, his boots gleamed, and he wore a new bowler tilted at a jaunty angle. "Good afternoon, Master Jeremy," he said, as Jeremy climbed onto the seat beside him.

"Good afternoon, Lester. The station, please."

"Certainly, sir. Gid'up there, Iris."

Iris tossed her head against the unfamiliar weight of the Fourth of July harness, making the medallions flash in the sun. She stepped off smartly, her head high, as if she, too, had taken to her role.

They crossed the Eau Claire and clopped up the hill toward the spires of Sacred Heart. They passed knots of lumberjacks striding toward the railroad station. The duffels on their shoulders came in a dozen colors and at least as many shapes. Often the handle of a trusted ax or peavey poked from the top or rode lashed to a side. "Where do you suppose they are?" Jeremy asked.

"I wouldn't know where your lowborn friends are, Master Jeremy. I would suggest, however, that finding your father is of greater consequence."

Jeremy looked at Lester hard, wondering if he'd taken too thoroughly to his role. But Lester winked at him and Jeremy laughed. "You know, you really would've made a good servant in one of those mansions."

"No, too much bowing and scraping. My people did that for a couple of hundred years and more. That's enough, I figure."

Jeremy hesitated. "Lester, were your parents slaves?"

"Sure enough. My pappy bought his freedom when he was twenty-six and fought for the North during the Civil War. But my mama had to wait until Father Abraham declared the slaves free."

"President Lincoln?"

"To Negroes born slaves, he was always Father Abraham, and that's the name I grew up hearing. My mama kept a picture of him in the living room. After my pappy died and she got old, she used to talk to it. Ask Father Abraham what she should do with this or that grandchild. What the weather was going to be and was it safe to plant her beans yet. And once or twice a day after the rheumatism started getting bad, she'd ask him when was the Lord going to come and take her." Lester laughed. "Yep, Father Abraham heard a lot of questions by the time she died. I always hoped that they had a chance to get together up yonder so that he could answer a few of them." He straightened. "There's the train whistle. Time we started remembering who we're supposed to be. You feeling yourself?"

"Not at all," Jeremy said.

Lester parked the buggy well back from the platform. The passing lumberjacks only glanced at the boy and the black man, although a few paused to admire Iris's harness. A half dozen men in dark suits and low-brimmed hats prowled the platform, eyeing the men. "There are the railroad detectives," Lester said. "They're taking their orders from those two men standing by the conductor. They must be from the company."

"The train's getting pretty full. Do you think I ought to do it now?"

"Wait a few minutes more. We want all the detectives to be able to see you. And we especially want those bigwigs to stop paying attention to anyone else."

Jeremy waited for what seemed the longest five minutes of his life. "Now," Lester said. "I'll be along soon as you need me."

Jeremy got out of the carriage and walked purposefully onto the platform. He felt men's stares, some curious, some amused, a few resentful. A big lumberjack being questioned by one of the detectives stared at Jeremy and then spat derisively. "Why don't you ask that rich kid what he's doing here and let an honest man get on with making a living?"

The detective looked at Jeremy. "Uh, son. Is there something I can help you with?"

It was his cue. Jeremy let out a bleat and ran to the side of the train. "Father! Father! Are you in there?" He jumped up, trying to peer through the open windows.

The lumberjacks milling about inside paused to stare at the dandified boy. They started laughing. "Hey, Carl," one yelled to another. "You this boy's pa?"

"Ain't mine. Maybe he's Caribou Bill's. Hey, Bill!"

The merriment spread as Jeremy kept jumping and bleating, "Father! Faatheer! Come out, Father!"

"Kid! Come here, kid!" The detective came hurrying after him to the even greater amusement of the lumberjacks.

Jeremy dodged the detective. He ran on to the next carriage and to the next, bouncing and bleating. Another detective tried to intercept him, but Jeremy ducked under his arm and ran to the next carriage, where he tried to wriggle in among the lumberjacks boarding the train. Good-naturedly, they pushed him back, but he persisted until one of them picked him up by the collar and set him back from the crowd. "You stay there, boy. Your daddy's not on this train." He looked at another lumberjack. "Boy must be a little touched."

The two detectives came panting up. "Who is this kid?" the older one growled. "Nobody dressed up rich like him is gonna have a pa on this train."

The younger one said, "Well, better not touch him rough. Now, son, you've got to keep back from the—"

But Jeremy had looked around the platform and seen that the other detectives were still busy surveying the thinning crowd of lumberjacks on the platform. He shot away, dodging through the crowd, and ran up and down beside the train, bleating, "Father! Where are you, Father? Father, it's Percival. Come out, Father!"

Soon most of the detectives were chasing him, but they were hesitant to grab him because of the fineness of his clothes. The hilarity of the lumberjacks increased every time Jeremy dodged one of the angry men. Finally, three of the detectives cornered him. "Now you boys be nice!" a lumberjack shouted from the train. "Ain't no cause to beat up on that kid."

The senior of the men from the company strode up, red faced and angry, his assistant trailing behind. It was then that Lester intervened, hurrying onto the platform and grabbing Jeremy's arm. "Master Percival! Now you stop. Your daddy is not on this train. You think real hard—like you used to be able to do—and you'll know that."

"What's going on here?" the red-faced man demanded.

Jeremy was trying to pull away from Lester, still squealing, "Father, Father." Real tears ran down his cheeks, although he couldn't imagine what had made them start falling.

"He's not quite right," Lester said, making a whirligig motion near his temple with a finger, at the same time trying to get control of the squirming boy. "His father was lost on the *Titanic*, but the boy won't believe it. He begs to come up here every day, expecting his daddy to be on—"

The man from the company had heard enough. He grabbed Jeremy by the collar. "Here, boy, you stop this ruckus!" And Jeremy, with all the anger he'd laid up over the fate of Willie and Eddie, with all the hatred he'd stored away over the attack on Murphy and Sven, and with altogether more pleasure than he would have thought possible, hauled off and kicked the man in the shins. The man roared and the lumberjacks cheered.

"You got 'em, little boss," one of them shouted. "And big boss, you'd better not lay another hand on him or you'll answer to about a hundred of us."

At the far end of the platform, Jeremy could see Uncle Mac standing, arms loose at his sides, helpless. Then, strolling across the platform, as unhurried and casual as if they were boarding a private Pullman car, came Soupy, Sven, and last of all, Murphy. They swung their duffels up to willing hands at the windows and climbed aboard. One foot on the step, Murphy raised a hand in salute and then disappeared into a throng of cheering, laughing men.

Jeremy stopped struggling to break free of Lester's grasp, straightened, and was about to announce that he felt quite better now and that, yes, he was ready to agree that his father couldn't be aboard this roughneck train after all. But all at once that seemed an overwhelming amount to say, and Jeremy took refuge in the time-honored, if somewhat undignified, act of feigning a faint.

Lester swept him up, delivering all the while a stream of excuses and apologies to the swearing company official, who was staggering about holding his shin, and fled the platform with Jeremy in his arms. Jeremy kept his eyes closed, but he heard the swell of cheers spreading the length of the train as the word passed that the great Murphy had made it aboard. Jeremy giggled against Lester's chest. "Hush," Lester hissed. "Wait until we're away from here. Then you can laugh all you want to."

Lester drew up the buggy two blocks from the station and turned to Jeremy, his eyes wide with wonder. "You are some actor, boy. Where'd you learn how to cry like that? You had me half convinced that you really had gone yappers."

"Nah, I ain't crazy yet." Jeremy looked back toward the depot, where he could see the first chuffs of steam as the engineer opened the throttle. The chuffs came faster and the train whistle let out a long, brave cry.

They watched the train cross the bridge over North Dewey Street. "Do you think we'll ever see them again?" Jeremy asked.

"Not most of 'em."

"But Murphy, Sven, and Soupy. They'll come back, won't they?"

Lester hesitated. "I wouldn't guess so, Jeremy. Except maybe Soupy. Murphy and Sven . . . Well, they'll go where there's still pine."

Jeremy watched until the last car disappeared around the bend and Lester started Iris for home. He kept his eyes averted so that Lester wouldn't see the real tears he had to blink away as the rattle of the train wheels faded and the whistle sounded a long final wail.

Chapter 11

☽

The addition of Beard & Lowe's wholesale customers to his regular list of calls kept Mr. Callahan on the road most of June, and Jeremy feared that work would force his father to break his promise of taking him to the Fourth of July fair. But at supper the evening before, he heard the downstairs door open and the thump of heavy sample cases on the floor of the hall.

He rushed down the steps and, forgetting the recent manly dignity of their relationship, threw his arms around his father. Mr. Callahan recovered his balance and, laughing, returned the hug. "So you're excited about the fair, eh?"

"And having you home, Pa. Are we still going up in the balloon?"

"Certainly. Now help me get these cases upstairs. I need some supper or I won't have the strength to go to the fair."

When Mr. Callahan was seated at the table with a plate of sausages and cabbage, he spoke loudly enough for Uncle Mac to hear. "Perhaps we'll even talk your great-uncle into flying. Old buzzard like him should be a natural at it."

Uncle Mac turned from the sink, where he was scraping the worst out of a frying pan so that Mrs. Higgins wouldn't complain when she did the supper dishes in the morning. "Old buzzard, am I? Well, better that than a preening popinjay like some I could mention."

"Touché. But will you go up in the balloon with us?"

Uncle Mac shook his head. "No, if man were meant to fly, he would have—"

"Been born with wings," Mr. Callahan finished. "I believe you've said that before."

"But you are going to the fair, aren't you?" Jeremy asked.

The old man shrugged. "If I have time. Right now the maiden takes most of my attention." He turned back to the frying pan.

Jeremy made a face and whispered to his father, "And mine, too. Even though I don't do much but sit."

His father put a finger to his lips. "So how is she coming?" he asked Uncle Mac.

"Slowly. Two-Horse and I spent most of today discussing her headdress."

"Meaning that they spent a long time just staring at her," Jeremy whispered.

"You can speak up, Jeremy," Uncle Mac said. "That's if you remember any of your manners."

"After I've eaten, I'll stroll over and have a look at her," Mr. Callahan said. "Maybe I can offer a suggestion or two. When I was Jeremy's age, a lot of the Chippewa women wore their finery to town on Saturdays. I think I remember the details pretty well."

"She's all covered up for the night," Uncle Mac growled.

Perhaps because he was tired from the trip, a look of irritation crossed Mr. Callahan's face. It was gone as quickly as it had come, and he smiled at Jeremy and shrugged. But Jeremy had seen the anger flash in his father's eyes.

Jeremy and his father rode a crowded trolley up Plank Hill to the fairgrounds on the bluff south of town. At every stop more families clambered aboard, swelling the crowd until Jeremy and his father clung laughing to the pole at the rear step.

Though later Jeremy would be able to recall nearly everything he saw, at first the fair seemed overwhelming. In a long gallery under the banner announcing THE AGE OF PETROLEUM, gasoline engines in a score of different sizes belched, thumped, roared, and sputtered, their attending salesman bellowing over the din how "the internal-combustion engine will soon make the buggy and the steam engine as obsolete as the ox cart and the waterwheel."

Farther along, the crowd pressed around the Ford sales-man, who rested an elbow proudly on the fender of a new Model T as he described how Ford would soon produce a thousand cars a day on its revolutionary assembly line in Dearborn, Michigan: "At a price of only six hundred dollars, Ford will bring the automobile within the grasp of every honest, hardworking family, business, and farm."

Jeremy nudged his father. "And Callahan's Sundries, huh?"

"Perhaps," Mr. Callahan said.

In a gallery across a strip of dusty street, THE WORLD OF ELECTRICITY promised an equally dazzling future. A salesman climbed atop a box to brag of the coming wonders: electric washing machines, electric carpet sweepers, electric ovens, even electric iceboxes. This last was too much for some in the crowd, who scoffed and turned away. "Just you wait!" the salesman shouted after them. "Electricity is the future. We have only begun to see its miracles."

"Let's look at the stock barns," Mr. Callahan said.

Jeremy cared little about cows when he could see inventions, but his father only laughed at his grousing and led the way. In a few minutes Jeremy forgot his reluctance. The farmers of the Chippewa Valley had wrought a miracle out of the ruin of the forest. With dynamite, workhorses, and muscle, they had cleared the stumps and boulders from the land. They had burned the brush, hitched up the plows, and made the land productive again. In the stock barns, prize Holsteins, Guernseys, Swiss, and Jerseys stood chewing their cuds and gazing at the gawkers in placid assurance of their right to inherit the land once roamed by wolf, bear, wolverine, and elk.

The exhibition hall beside the stock barns held a thousand examples of the hard work of the farming families: honey, maple syrup, jellies, jams, preserves, and pickles; cakes, pies, breads, and cookies; quilts, blankets, and rugs; embroidery, tatting, needlepoint, knitting, and crochet. A young woman turned from inspecting a quilt and Jeremy recognized Nancy Two-Horse in bonnet and Sunday dress, her teeth flashing as she laughed up into the face of a young man. Jeremy felt a twist of his heart so painful that he was sure it must have broken.

Perhaps the sunlight from the open doors dazzled her vision and made Jeremy into a featureless silhouette. Or perhaps she just didn't think to recognize a boy of so little consequence in her life as they swept by him and into the sunshine.

"Say," Jeremy's father said. "Wasn't that the young Indian woman Uncle Mac has posing for his statue?"

"Yes."

"I should have touched my hat, but she caught me by surprise. Handsome fellow with her. Looked at least some Indian."

Jeremy didn't respond but made a show of inspecting a table covered with embroidery, seeing nothing.

It was well into the afternoon when Jeremy and his father emerged from the last of the exhibitions. They ate sausages and sauerkraut and then wandered through the carnival, past the merry-go-round, the miniature railroad, the games of chance, and the freak show.

Beyond the carnival lay a wide field where a towering, striped balloon ascended and descended on a thick cable. When Mr. Callahan paused to listen to a speaker extolling the virtues of the Democratic candidate for president, Jeremy pulled at his sleeve. "Pa, there's the balloon. Come on."

"You go ahead. I'm interested in hearing about this Woodrow Wilson. Get a place in line and I'll join you."

The balloon rose on its cable, the tall wicker basket swinging with the weight of six people. Jeremy clutched the rail and peered over the side, his heart hammering. His father squeezed his shoulder. "Look over there, you can see all the way to Caryville."

"And up there's Chippewa Falls! Imagine how far you could see from an airplane, Pa!" His father laughed and held tighter to Jeremy's shoulder as the balloon hit the top of the cable and the basket swayed.

For far too short a time, they swung there. From on high, the fair and even the city seemed tiny, while the land stretched on forever. Jeremy could see the farms laid out, their green patchwork stitched by streams and country roads. Piles of stumps and brush burned in twisting knots of smoke that thickened the afternoon haze so the horizon seemed gauzy. And through it all ran the meandering ribbon of the great river that had emptied the north of trees and now—save for the thinning fabric of logs above the catch boom—flowed on, an uninterrupted blue, toward the southwestern horizon and the Mississippi. And Jeremy's heart, so recently broken, swelled with possibility.

Chapter 12

☽

In the week after the fair, dogs panted in the shade and horses standing in harness let their heads droop almost to the pavement. Jeremy worried about Eddie and Willie working in the hellish heat of the boiler room as log after log from the Chippewa disappeared into the racketing fury of the mill.

He went every morning to the shop, but there was even less to do than before. Uncle Mac had stopped carving and sat with Two-Horse through the days under the big maple, the two of them drinking coffee despite the heat and rising only to move their chairs to stay in the shade. Perhaps it was just too hot to work, but Jeremy sensed that the two old men were waiting for some signal that would tell them it was time to finish the maiden.

In the heat only Arlyn was busier, as he shaved ice and slid cold drinks across the counter at the soda fountain in Callahan's. The counter was half full of men on a Wednesday when Jeremy offered to help, but Arlyn was protective of his narrow territory behind the counter: "No, you'll do the job better than me and then I'll be out of one.

Here, let me jerk you a soda and then you can run along and find your friends."

Jeremy leaned on the counter, making the soda last until nothing but a single sliver of ice remained. He tilted the glass back, trying to get the sliver to slide down the side. "Here, give this boy another soda if he's that parched. I'll have one with him." Hans Weister slapped a dime on the counter.

"Yes, sir," Arlyn said. "Do you want one, Jeremy?"

"Of course he wants one," Weister said. He leaned toward Jeremy, his breath stinking of whiskey. "So, young Jeremy, what's that old coot McAlester and that greasy pal of his doing over there, anyway? I hear rumor that they got themselves a magic log and they're carving a beyoutiful Injun maiden."

Several of the other men chuckled.

"I'm sorry, but I can't say, Mr. Weister," Jeremy said.

"You mean you don't know? Or you just ain't saying?"

"I know, but I just can't say."

By some sleight of hand, a shiny quarter appeared in Weister's fingers. He flipped it high above the counter so that it glittered in the sunlight flooding through the store windows. He caught it between thumb and forefinger, then held it out to Jeremy. "It's been my experience over long years of dealing with the human race that all secrets have their price."

The soda fountain was suddenly hushed. Jeremy felt himself mesmerized by the shiny coin, and his hand moved of its own accord to take it. Then he looked Weister in the eye. "Not this one," he said.

Arlyn, who'd been shifting nervously from foot to foot, suddenly began wiping the counter with his towel. "Little bit sticky here, Mr. Weister. Let me wipe it before you get something on your sleeve. Would you like a sandwich to go with that soda?"

Jeremy turned from the counter, leaving his second soda untouched. Weister called after him, "How's that Injun girl mixed up in this? I've had my eye on her."

A sudden redness clouded Jeremy's vision, but he spoke levelly. "I really can't say, Mr. Weister."

He crossed the street, the anger seething in him. Uncle Mac and Two-Horse sat in their accustomed places beneath the maple. Jeremy stood in front of them, hands on hips. "Uncle Mac, why aren't you working on the maiden? If you'll let me, I'll help. But I can't wait around anymore!"

Uncle Mac raised his eyebrows and then looked at Two-Horse. The old Indian nodded. Without a word, Uncle Mac rose and led the way into the shop. He handed Jeremy a chisel and a mallet. "You can start here, below the hem of her dress, where the calf rounds into the wood. Go slow, and call me when you don't know how much to cut away. Remember, anything you cut off won't go back on again."

He turned from Jeremy, selected a thin chisel and a small mallet, and studied the maiden's face. He grunted and started working. In the far corner of the shop, Two-Horse settled himself in the shadows, a faint smile creasing the corners of his mouth.

Jeremy was so intent on his work that he hardly noticed the storm coming until the afternoon light went dim and the first thunder rumbled in the west. He looked up then, surprised to feel a cool breeze coming through the open door of the shop. "Rain," Uncle Mac said. "We're through the heat."

Jeremy spotted Willie from the window of Professor Hauenstein's piano studio. "A friend?" the professor asked.

"Uh, yes, sir. I haven't seen him in a while. A long while." He looked into the professor's kindly eyes. "Could we finish this piece next time?"

"Of course. You did vell today. Go see your friend."

Jeremy hurried across the street still damp from the rain of the night before. Willie seemed to be prowling in thought along the sidewalk in front of Callahan's. "Willie!" Jeremy called.

Willie looked around. His eyes were hollow and red rimmed, his skin gray with dirt, dried sweat, and fatigue. "Hello, Jeremy," he said, his voice hoarse.

"Willie, are you okay? You look terrible."

Willie shrugged. "Oh, I'm all right. I did a double shift and I ain't washed or eaten yet. Soap, food, and a little sleep, that's all I need."

The two friends stood a pace apart, awkward and unable to begin. Jeremy felt pitifully young, distanced from this older Willie by an immense span of experience and suffering. "Where's Eddie? Is he okay?"

"I wish I knew. I came to ask if he'd come by to see you before he left town. Didn't say nothin' to the rest of us. Just lit a shuck for somewhere."

"He never came by here. When did he go?"

"Four days ago. Same day Pa got back from spreeing away everything they collected for him down at the mill. Took him three days to sleep off the booze, and he would have taken another if Weister hadn't made him go to work collecting bills. Doubt Pa's even noticed that Eddie's gone."

"Maybe Eddie just needed a chance to think. I bet he'll be back just as soon—"

"Nah, he's gone for good. He would've told somebody if he planned on coming back. You as likely as any. . . . Well, I gotta go. I'm on shift again tonight." He started down the sidewalk.

"Willie, can't you stay? We could go upstairs, and I could get you something to eat. Then you could use the bathtub and maybe take a nap."

Willie hesitated a moment, but then shook his head. "Nah, I really gotta go. We'll see you sometime."

In his desperation to make him stay, Jeremy blurted, "How's Agnes?"

Willie turned, surprised. "Agnes? I don't know. She don't say much these days. Not that she ever said a lot except to swear and yell at us. She tried to make friends with the fancy girls on Water Street, but they wouldn't have anything to do with her."

"I'm sorry."

"That a bunch of fancy girls wouldn't take up with her?" Willie laughed. "Well, I guess you'd feel sorry for anybody." He turned and, with a shake of his head, trudged toward the bridge to the West Side.

✳ ✳ ✳

At times Jeremy wondered at himself for insisting on helping with the carving. He wielded the mallet and chisel hesitantly, afraid that too hard a blow might gouge away a deep sliver that would forever ruin all the careful work. Uncle Mac reassured him, showed him how to position the chisel and to strike it just so with the mallet. They rotated the statue on the big bolts resting in the sawhorses. Jeremy started working on the back of the torso while Uncle Mac gave the final shape to the legs.

Often now, Jeremy spent the entire day in the shop. The statue had become a "she" to him as the maiden emerged gracefully from the pine. Uncle Mac had left the beam uncarved behind the ankles and neck to preserve strength as the statue became thinner elsewhere. By the end of another week, all but those two places and her face, hair, and headdress were ready to sand.

Jeremy went to bed feeling tired and forlorn that Friday night. His father had been in La Crosse since the fair and had wired that he would need another week to put things right at Beard & Lowe's warehouse.

He awoke deep in the night, unsure what had disturbed his sleep. A pebble rattled against the window. He hurried to peer into the alley. Had Eddie come back? Or perhaps it was Willie, intent on some late-night adventure. He peered into the dimness. The figure waving at him was small, but it was neither of the Cripshank twins. Jeremy slid the window up. "Soupy?"

The figure bobbed his head and gestured toward the street.

"You want me to come down?"

Soupy nodded rapidly and finally spoke. "Please. It's Murphy needs you."

Jeremy pulled on clothes and tiptoed down the stairs, putting on his shoes when he reached the back door. In the alley, Soupy grabbed his arm and pulled him into the shadows. "Soupy, what is it? What are you doing back here?" Jeremy whispered.

With great effort after so much silence, Soupy spoke. "They beat us up. Ambushed us. Company goons. A few of the boys joined in on our side, but they had us good. They hurt Murphy bad. And Sven . . ." He hesitated.

"What about Sven?"

"Sven caught a peavey upside the head. Killed him." Jeremy felt his legs go weak. Soupy's hand tightened on his arm. "They kept Murphy in jail and wouldn't take him to a doc. I got together what money we had and borrowed the rest and paid his fine. But I knew the goons would kill him if they caught up with us. So I got him on a freight headed east. Took us two weeks to get here."

"Should I get Dr. Curtis?"

Soupy shook his head. "No! They'll kill Murphy if they catch him here. It's the same company, and they always got goons. I need to get him to my farm down in Durand. I can take care of him there. Old Doc Evans'll come and never say nothin'. That's why I come to you. Figured you could talk to that black friend of yours. Get him to help us."

"Where's Murphy?"

"Up in the rail yards. I left him with a couple of tramps. They seemed okay, and we ain't got nothin' to steal anyway."

"I'll get Uncle Mac."

"We don't want to get no one in trouble. I mean you's a boy and if—"

"Uncle Mac doesn't care about trouble. Not for you guys."

Lester hitched Buzz and Iris to a light wagon and held their heads while Uncle Mac helped Soupy into the back of the wagon. Soupy hadn't complained to Jeremy about his knee, but it was hugely swollen and the lumberjack winced in pain. "The goons do this to you?" Jeremy asked.

Soupy, done with more speech than necessary, shook his head. "Jumping from a train." He made a tumbling motion with a hand and smiled. Lester stepped back from the horses, and Uncle Mac slapped the reins.

The tramps had a small fire going beneath a tin can, and one of them was trying to spoon soup into Murphy's shattered mouth. "He was in a bad way with the shivers," the tramp said. "Thought he could stand some soup."

"I'm obliged," Soupy said. He gestured toward Uncle Mac and Jeremy. "These are friends."

The tramps nodded. The one who'd spoken moved aside so that Uncle Mac could kneel in front of Murphy. He pushed back the long hair that hid Murphy's face, and Jeremy had to look away. Uncle Mac murmured, "Oh, they have done their worst this time, Brother Murphy."

For a moment it did not seem that the big man heard, but then he lifted a hand and squeezed Uncle Mac's arm, as if comforting him. He did not open his eyes.

"He's blind," Soupy said quietly. "Ever since the fight."

The tramp who'd spoken looked nervously at the sky. "You'd better get him out of here. It's gonna be light soon. Me and Harry gonna hike out to Altoona and try to catch a freight there. Don't pay to stick around here. The railroad dicks hereabouts always had a bad reputation, but they've gotten even meaner since some kid made fools of 'em a month or so ago."

Uncle Mac nodded. "Heard tell as much." He dug in a pocket and handed a dollar to each of the men. "Good luck to you men. Better tomorrows."

They touched their caps. The silent one kicked out the fire while the other helped Uncle Mac get Murphy to his feet. "Come on, Murph," Soupy said, and took his arm. The big man followed, head hanging, his sightless gaze on his feet.

Jeremy could think of nothing to say as they set off across town in the early light. They crossed the Chippewa on the Madison Street Bridge to avoid being seen near the mills. A heavy young woman was leaning on the downstream railing, elbows bent and chin on hands, watching the river passing below. Jeremy recognized her and turned away quickly. Agnes.

When they were nearly to the end of the bridge, he chanced a look back. She was staring after them with the smoking rage that always seemed to possess her.

It took them half the day to reach the farm west of Durand. Soupy's wife and daughter greeted him offhandedly, as if he had merely gone to town. But they were kind to Murphy.

The daughter went to fetch the doctor while Uncle Mac and Soupy's wife helped the big man up to bed.

Soupy sat on the porch with a rag and the basin of cold well water his wife had given him to bathe his swollen knee. Jeremy sat beside him. At last, Soupy looked up to survey the farm. He smiled at Jeremy, a little sadly but with something of the old amusement in his eyes. "I'm home now, I guess."

"For good?"

He nodded, still smiling. "I cut some trees and done my part for the workingman as well as I was able. Time to be a farmer." He shrugged. "Worse things. But I will miss the trees." He wrung out the rag and bathed his knee again, done talking.

When the doctor had come and gone, Uncle Mac offered a small fold of bills to Soupy's wife. The woman hesitated. "Take it," Uncle Mac said. "You will have the care of him, the money is little to that."

She nodded and took it. "Would you and the boy stay the night?"

"No, better that we get back." Passing Soupy, he laid a hand on his shoulder. "Good-bye, my friend. We'll come again."

Soupy bobbed his head. He smiled at Jeremy.

When they were a distance from the farm, Jeremy asked, "What'd the doctor say, Uncle Mac?"

"That Murphy will live. What manner of life is harder to say. He's blind, he's lost the hearing in one ear, and he remembers that he is Murphy but little else. Only time will tell if he gets any of that back. But he's safe now. Here, lean against me for a while and rest."

Jeremy leaned against him and watched the bobbing heads of the horses until he felt his own head starting to nod and he slept.

Lester and Two-Horse sat in front of the livery stable in the soft July night. Uncle Mac climbed down stiffly, and Jeremy scrambled after him. "Thank you, Lester," Uncle Mac said. "Charge me for extra oats for the horses. They've had a long day."

While Lester unhitched the wagon and led the horses inside, Uncle Mac stretched the kinks out of his joints. "How is the big Irish?" Two-Horse asked.

"No worse than can be expected. And no better."

Jeremy followed the two old men across Barstow and up River Street toward home. A breeze brought the smells of the town and the river. The last trolley of the evening clanged across the Grand Avenue Bridge, its lights reflected in the dark water below. "The town is getting quieter," Uncle Mac said. "Now the lumberjacks are gone, it will be a very different place."

"Yes," Two-Horse said. "We are coming to the end of many things."

"Go to bed, Jeremy. I'm going to look in on the maiden. Perhaps work on her face a little. I may see something by the light of a lamp that I haven't been able to see in daylight."

"Then I'll come, too."

Uncle Mac hesitated. "All right. But only to watch. I don't want you handling a sharp chisel this late at night."

Jeremy curled up in the old stuffed chair next to Two-Horse's corner. Uncle Mac worked slowly on the maiden's face, pausing a long time between gentle taps with the mallet on the chisel. Jeremy shifted in the chair to stay awake, but soon Uncle Mac's movements in the yellow light became hypnotic and he let his eyes close.

He awoke at the touch of Uncle Mac's hand on his knee. "Come look," Uncle Mac said. He led Jeremy to the maiden.

Jeremy sucked in his breath when he saw what Uncle Mac had brought out of the wood. The maiden lay as if dreaming, her face serene in the knowledge of things ancient and unseen. The unpainted face had the cool loveliness of marble, beautiful but somehow chilling. "She's beautiful, Uncle Mac," Jeremy managed. "You found her at last."

"I was only a little of the doing. Like Two-Horse promised, she came to us. I felt her tonight in the breeze from the river, and I knew it was time to finish." He picked up a small square of sandpaper and smoothed a rough spot on her cheek.

Jeremy looked about. "Where is he?"

"When I finished, he came to look. He told me that it was good, then I think he went off to thank whatever it is he prays to. Lately he's been spending his nights on the bluff beyond Little Niagara. He told me there's a cave up there where he can sit looking at the river. And if he sits long enough, he can sometimes forget that white men ever came to this land." He brushed sawdust away from the maiden's eyes and stepped back.

Together they stared at her for a long time. "Are you going to give her a name?" Jeremy asked.

"I will call her Crescent Moon because she will be young like the new moon long after Two-Horse and I and all the rest of our kind are gone."

"Please don't talk that way, Uncle Mac," Jeremy said.

Uncle Mac smiled sadly. "All things pass away. Only the love in the work lives on. It's a small thing, even a puny thing sometimes, but it's all we have to fight the ugliness of what some men will do to the land or to men like Murphy." He turned down the kerosene lamp until it flickered and then gently blew out the flame. "Come. The night has a couple of hours yet, and we need to sleep."

Chapter 13

☽

With only the strengthening blocks behind the neck and ankles uncarved, Jeremy and Uncle Mac began sanding Crescent Moon. Sanding had always seemed drudgery before, but Jeremy took pleasure in it now. The roughness left by the chisel blades fell away until the wood shone smooth and white as if lit by a gentle light within.

After three days the sanding was nearly done. Two-Horse ate dinner with them above Callahan's. Mrs. Higgins sniffed in disapproval at the sight of him but served them without further comment.

Jeremy finished quickly and returned to the shop. He'd just begun sanding again when he felt a weight of air displaced behind him. He turned to find Hans Weister, sweat gleaming on his fat, grinning face. At his elbow stood Mr. Cripshank, thin and haggard, looking shaky for the want of whiskey. "Ah, so here is the great mystery," Weister drawled. He stepped closer. "And a pretty thing she is." He nudged the smaller man. "How would you like to meet her in the flesh, Cripshank? Catch her in a dark place where she couldn't object to a little male friendliness?"

Jeremy jumped to his feet, blocking the big man from coming any closer. "Mr. Weister, the shop is closed. It's been closed for weeks and weeks." He looked frantically about for the sheet to pull over Crescent Moon.

"Relax, boy. I just came by to be neighborly. Besides, I just might need a wooden figure of my own while there is still someone who can carve them. Perhaps I might even be interested in this one."

"As my nephew told you, the shop is closed," Uncle Mac said from the door. "We are taking no orders, and this figure is not for sale. If you have anything to say to me, come into the street."

"Why, McAlester! Would you make a man stand in the hot sun?"

"There is shade by the shop."

Weister shrugged and winked at Jeremy. "Well, another time then. I would not interrupt a man at his work. Or a *boy*." He laughed. "Come, Cripshank. We'll go see if we can convince some of your neighbors to remember their debts."

Uncle Mac glared after them, then picked up a sanding block. "He's a bad man, Jeremy. If it weren't for his size, someone would have dealt with him long ago." He started sanding the neck and shoulders of Crescent Moon.

Jeremy returned to sanding the legs. After a few minutes, he asked, "Why does he have Mr. Cripshank following him around?"

Uncle Mac snorted. "To make himself feel like a lion. But Weister will never be a lion even if he does have his jackal now."

Near dusk, Jeremy went fishing along the edge of the logs. They had once covered the river from the catch boom to the mouth of the Eau Claire and beyond, but a summer of sawing had thinned them until now they were thick only between the bridge at Water Street and the catch boom. Most of the mills no longer ran shifts around the clock, and only the great saws of Valley One still screamed through the night.

When he still hadn't gotten a bite after half an hour, Jeremy crossed the river at Water Street and fished upstream to the railroad bridge. He climbed the embankment and stood at the point where the earth fell away and the ties marched out onto the iron skeleton of the bridge.

He had promised his father never to cross the railroad bridge, but he was tired and the bridge was the shortest way home. He stepped out onto the ties, counting them, reaching a dozen, then twenty. From the shore, it had seemed the simplest thing in the world to walk blithely across the pine ties, but every step forced him to look into the gaps between them, where there was nothing but the long drop to the swirling water below. He kept counting, kept trying not to look. On shore, he'd noticed only a breeze, but here a wind blew, thrumming in the iron girders so that the ties themselves seemed to vibrate.

He retreated on shaking legs, thankful for once that he did not have the companionship of Willie and Eddie, who were immensely braver and would have hooted at his fear. He walked up stream to cross the river on the concrete and steel safety of the Grand Avenue Bridge, reaching the east side in the early dark.

He was only a block from home, walking with his pole on his shoulder, when a powerful hand pulled him into an alley and threw him against a wall so that his forehead smacked the brick. Agnes pinned him there, leaning over his shoulder, her hot, sour breath on his cheek. "Hello, Jeremy. What've you got for Agnes?"

He tried to worm away, but her grip was like a vise. "Come on, Agnes. What do you want?"

She laughed harshly. "Money. That's what everybody wants, ain't it? I had some, had almost enough to get out of this stinking town, but Pa found it and drank it up. So now I got to start earning it again. And I figured why not go see a little rich boy name of Jeremy Callahan? He might pay to keep me from telling some things I seen."

"I ain't rich."

She snorted. "That's not what I hear down on Water Street. I hear that your pa's buying this and he's buying that. He's got new stores all over."

"He doesn't. All he bought was a warehouse in La Crosse."

She banged him against the wall again. "I don't care what he bought! I know you got money, and you're going to give me some or I'm gonna tell how I saw you and old McAlester taking that big Wobbly out of town in a wagon. Him and that little one who never talks. The big one'd been beaten around something terrible. I'll bet there's them that'd pay lots to find him so they could finish the job."

"They blinded him, Agnes! God, can't you feel sorry for him and keep quiet?"

"Sorry for him? Since when does Agnes Cripshank have time to feel sorry for anybody? I got my own problems." She shook him. "So you got money for me, little rich boy? Or shall I find someone else to pay me?"

"I don't have much, but I'll give you what I've got. But you've got to promise not to tell about Murphy."

"Murphy." She rolled the word around. "Yeah, I remember the name now. Big Murphy. What's the little one's name?"

"I don't remember."

"Oh, yes, you do. And I suspect it'd be real handy for me to know." She grabbed his wrist and started twisting it up behind his back. "You want that I should get it out of you?"

"Just let me give you the money, Agnes!"

"How much?"

"I've got six dollars and thirty cents."

"That all? Don't sound like much for Big Murphy's life. Why don't you just tell me the little one's name and where you took the two of 'em?" She twisted harder.

"Wait a second! I've . . . I've got a ten-dollar gold piece that was my mother's."

"More like it." She let go of his wrist and took him by the collar. "Let's go. And no tricks, brat. Or I swear I'll hurt you bad."

He jerked away, found his fishing pole in the dark, and set off for home without looking back.

∗ ∗ ∗

A light shone from under Uncle Mac's door. "I'm home," Jeremy called.

"Catch anything?"

"Nothing to keep. I'll be right back."

"Where are you going? It's getting late."

"Just to give a friend something. A fishing bait. It'll just take a minute."

He found Agnes waiting in the shadow of the big maple by the shop. He gave her the paper money and silver. "Where's the gold?" she growled.

He ran his thumb over the smooth, buttery warmth of the coin and then held it out to her. "Here."

She snatched it and held it up to the pale light from the window of Jensen's Boardinghouse and Travelers' Inn. She grunted with pleasure and put it into her dress. Jeremy wished that he had something to hit her with—a club or a length of board or a fist-size rock—but he spoke evenly. "And you won't tell. You've got to promise you won't tell. If your pa knew, he'd—"

She laughed at him. "Do you think I'm stupid enough to take a gold coin home so Pa can steal it? No, Agnes is gonna be on the morning train. And you and this whole stinking town can go to the devil."

Uncle Mac carefully cut away the strengthening blocks behind Crescent Moon's neck and ankles. "We'll smooth those spots later. Now I want to get her standing."

They ran ropes under her shoulders and knees to support her weight. Uncle Mac cut away the uncarved beam between her head and the sawhorse. Then, as Jeremy held

123

his breath, he cut away the beam at the other end, leaving only enough of it for a stand. With Two-Horse's help, they eased her from the rope cradle and gently tilted her upright so that she stood for the first time. Uncle Mac walked around her critically. "Good," he muttered. "Very good."

Though her balance seemed perfect to Jeremy, Uncle Mac insisted on bolting the stand to the floor. That done, they set about getting her ready to paint. Two-Horse prowled along the workbench on the far side of the shop, staring into paint jars, rejecting some colors immediately and spending long minutes studying others. Occasionally, he would bring a jar to show Uncle Mac, who would dip a sliver of pine into the paint and hold it at one point or another on Crescent Moon. Then, if they agreed, Two-Horse would set the jar aside.

Uncle Mac smiled at Jeremy. "Tomorrow we'll start painting. Then she'll have life. Now she is too cold."

Jeremy returned the smile, happy to know that Uncle Mac, too, had felt the coldness that needed to be warmed away with color.

When they were cleaning up, Uncle Mac said, "Oh, I meant to tell you. Old Fitch saw that rat in the basement. He had a fit, said one of these days it'd get in the store and ruin the business forever. Run down to the hardware store and get a better trap. I'll finish here."

Supper was on the table when Jeremy got back from the hardware store. He went fishing afterward and then lingered over a new penny thriller until well past eleven, when he finally remembered the rat trap. He hurried to the basement to set it.

He had just positioned it on one of the rat's usual paths through the crates and boxes when a board creaked above him in the store. He listened and heard another soft footfall. A chill went through him. What could Arlyn, Mr. Fitch, or Uncle Mac be doing in the store at this hour? Perhaps his father had returned ahead of schedule. But no, he wouldn't move stealthily in his own store. Jeremy edged up the stairs, moving carefully so that his weight wouldn't cause the steps to creak. The door into the store stood ajar, and he peered inside. A thin figure, seeming for a moment more shadow than man, knelt in a patch of moonlight. He was searching through the wrapping paper, string, and miscellaneous odds and ends on the shelves beneath the dry goods counter. Beside him on the floor stood a watchman's lantern, its door cracked so that a narrow beam of light leaked out. The man turned slightly, and Jeremy saw Mr. Cripshank's haggard, unshaven face.

Cripshank cursed under his breath and dug in the bottom shelf. Again he cursed, this time more vehemently. He lifted the lantern with a bandaged hand, swinging the beam recklessly around the room. "Where the devil . . ." he muttered.

Jeremy knew the answer to the unfinished question. The cash box was not in the store at all. Anyone who lingered at closing might see Mr. Fitch placing the day's receipts into the box beneath the counter. What the lingerer would not see was Uncle Mac coming down after supper to take the cash box upstairs to the safety of the apartment.

Cripshank must have guessed the answer, because he suddenly strode to the foot of the stairs. He dug something from a pocket and Jeremy heard a click and saw the blade of a clasp knife glinting in the light of the lantern. Jeremy tried to cry out then, to yell for all he was worth to wake Uncle Mac. But before he could gather the breath and the courage, Cripshank hesitated, losing whatever resolution whiskey and desperation had given him. For a long moment he stood breathing heavily. Then he rushed to a display case, threw back the sliding doors, and began stuffing his pockets with whatever came to his one good hand.

Jeremy knew that Cripshank could not have chosen worse. In the case to the right were silver-trimmed combs, brushes, and hand mirrors; in the case to the left, suede and patent-leather gloves, many of them imported from Italy. But Cripshank had chosen the case of discontinued, slightly defective, or simply odd items that Mr. Fitch thought beneath the dignity of the store to sell at all, but that Jeremy's father marked down to almost nothing so that young men not yet established could afford some gift for sweethearts or mothers.

His pockets stuffed, Cripshank bolted through the side door to the alley. Jeremy hurried to peer down the dim street after him. Cripshank was striding toward the railroad bridge, his feet seeming to fight the urge to run with every step. And for reasons that he would never be able to explain to himself, no matter how many times in later life he thought of that night, Jeremy followed.

✳ ✳ ✳

Cripshank was already halfway across the bridge, the echo of his steps rebounding against the iron framework, when Jeremy stepped out onto the ties. In the moonlight, the river roiled against the piers far below, tugging with its ceaseless, patient strength to tear away all that obstructed it. Like every boy who'd grown up by the river, Jeremy could read the Chippewa's changing moods, could feel this night its impatience with the bridge and all the things of man that even momentarily distracted it from its journey to the sea. But the same inexplicable impulse that had made him follow Cripshank from the store led him out onto the vibrating wood and iron over the dark, swirling water.

Cripshank had disappeared from sight by the time Jeremy reached the far shore, but he could hear the retreating scuff of boots. He hurried and caught sight of the man's hunched figure. Cripshank must have felt safe in the narrow streets of the West Side, because he moved without stealth, never looking back. Jeremy followed a few dozen paces behind, keeping to the shadows, until Cripshank turned off Niagara onto Third. When Jeremy reached the corner, he had disappeared again, this time completely. Had he sensed a pursuer and slipped into an alley or a yard? Perhaps he had caught a glimpse of Jeremy and even now crouched in ambush with his clasp knife.

Jeremy hesitated, and it was then that he heard voices. He moved cautiously along a picket fence, its slats like yellowed teeth in the moonlight. Cripshank was whining. "I got what I could, Hans. I searched and searched for the cash box, but old McAlester must take it upstairs. But I got good stuff. Here, just look."

Jeremy caught sight of the two men, their shadows outlined on the paint-flaked wall of a decrepit house. "Junk!" Weister snarled. "Absolute trash." He struck Cripshank's hand and the trinkets flew. "If you had the brains to blow your head off, you wouldn't have taken anything! Then we could have gone back another time for the cash box. But now they're going to be watching." He shoved the smaller man hard in the chest. "You're an imbecile, Cripshank. A sodden, sniveling fool, and I'm fed up with you. Get your old woman, your dirty brats, and your stinking carcass out of my house tomorrow! I'll rent it to someone who can pay me."

Jeremy saw the shadow of Weister's hand, gigantic against the wall, as the big man struck Cripshank on the side of the head. Cripshank went down and came up with the clasp knife in his hand. He lunged at Weister, who threw up an arm to block the thrust and howled as the blade sliced through the fatty part of his arm above the elbow. He clouted Cripshank, pitching him back against the wall and sending the knife flying. He closed his huge hands around Cripshank's neck, and the two men struggled, their shadows writhing on the wall, until Cripshank went limp.

Jeremy ran, his feet scrabbling on the gravel. Weister spun, his face bloated with rage in the moonlight. "You, boy!" he shouted. He cast Cripshank's body aside and scooped up the knife.

Jeremy could hear the pounding of the big man's feet in the street behind him. He ran faster, air tearing at his lungs, heart slamming in his chest. He dodged once into an alley to hide in the shadows, but when Weister turned the corner, unerring in his pursuit like some great beast guided more by scent than sight, he abandoned his hiding place and ran for the railroad bridge.

On the grade to the west, he heard the thudding chuff of a locomotive and the long wail of a whistle as a late-night freight plunged through the outskirts, intent on the river crossing. From long practice, he could tell by the rhythm of steel wheels on the tracks that the train had the highball, its engineer pushing his locomotive as fast as he dared over the cross streets toward the bridge and the long climb out of town to the east.

Behind him Weister shouted hoarsely, "Give it up, boy. Stop and we'll talk. I won't hurt you."

Jeremy ran faster. He scrambled up the railroad embankment, tossing a look behind him to see if he'd gained, but saw Weister clambering up behind him. The locomotive swung around the last bend before the river, its headlight bouncing off the houses along the tracks. Jeremy sprinted onto the bridge, the ribs of its iron skeleton rising on either side. The locomotive's whistle screamed. The ties flew by beneath his feet, the gaps between a plunging dark-ness. The locomotive's light washed over him, illuminating the gleaming rails, and the whistle screamed again as all around him the bridge shook. He looked behind and saw Weister standing beside the tracks, head thrown back, his laughter lost in the whistle's scream. The locomotive roared onto the bridge, smoke and sparks blasting from its stack, its blackness blacker than any night behind the merciless glare of its great eye. *Now*, Jeremy thought, and threw himself on the ties, letting his legs fall through the gap between. With a squeeze he pushed himself through until he fell into the cool, tarry air beneath the bridge.

He hung there, hands gripping the tie as the locomotive thundered overhead. He knew that he could not keep his grip, knew that the bone-rattling vibration would shake loose his puny hands. Yet he hung on, waiting until the last possible second before letting go to plunge blindly into the darkness. With luck, he would hit deep water, missing logs, pilings, and the wreck of the barge that had lain for a quarter of a century downstream of the bridge. Then the river would choose whether to drown him with whirlpool, undertow, or implacable current, or to hurl him against the shore within reach of an overhanging branch or a narrow beach.

Then suddenly, miraculously, the caboose clattered over, and the terrible vibration ceased. His arms had gone numb, and his muscles shrieked when he strained upward. He clawed at the tie, his fingernails digging for a better grip. He heaved his head and shoulders through the crack until he could rest for a moment on his elbows. Only then did he remember Weister and turn his head to look down the tracks.

The big man was coming slowly, his wounded arm hanging. He was babbling from loss of blood or exertion or perhaps insanity. He hissed, laughed, chuckled, spat strings of words. Then he spotted Jeremy and let out a howl more terrible than any sound Jeremy had ever heard.

Jeremy lunged through the gap and onto the bridge. He tried to get his feet under him, stumbled, got his balance, and ran. Ahead another figure reared up out of the darkness. And despite Weister's rapid footfalls behind him,

Jeremy hesitated for the briefest of seconds before running toward the figure with all his might. He stumbled on the last tie of the bridge and sprawled beyond Two-Horse's legs.

Two-Horse didn't so much as look down but raised his arms, palms outward. Weister laughed, the hard meanness returned to his voice, replacing the terrible babbling. "So, old chief. How do you plan to stop me? An Injun spell? The boy is mine. I'm gonna scalp him and throw him in the river. But you first." He lifted Cripshank's clasp knife, the bloody blade flashing.

It was then that Lester stepped from behind the bridge abutment and hit Weister with a two-by-four across the chest. The big man stumbled back, arms flailing for balance, and when Lester hit him a second time, the blow caught the knife hand and drove the blade into his chest. Weister dropped to his knees, staring dumbly at the protruding handle of the knife. Slowly, he raised a hand to pull it free. Lester hit him a third time then, aiming at the knife like he was driving a spike, and when Weister fell on his face, Jeremy could see that the blow had driven the blade clear through his back.

"Come," said Two-Horse, and took his arm.

Jeremy looked back as Two-Horse led him away. Lester tossed the two-by-four over the side of the bridge into the river. He tugged at the knife, pulled it free, and threw it after the board. Then carefully, almost gently, he arranged Weister's body on the tracks. In the distance Jeremy heard the first chuff of a westbound freight picking up speed as it cleared the yards.

Chapter 14

☽

Jeremy's father read from the newspaper:

"The bloody deaths of two city men resulted from a violent argument over stolen property, according to local police. Apparently, Edward R. Cripshank, an unemployed sawmill worker of spotted reputation, broke into Callahan's Sundries, 302 South River Street, some time in the late evening of July 28.

"Cripshank took his loot, described by Myron Fitch, store manager, as trinkets of little value, to the West Side. There he met Hans Weister, a notorious local character, in an alley off Third Avenue, a half block north of Water Street. Whether the encounter was by prearrangement or chance is uncertain, but the two engaged in a fight over the goods, wherein Cripshank was dispatched with blows and strangulation.

"Wounded in the set-to and leaving a marked effusion of blood with each step, Weister attempted to cross the railroad bridge over the Chippewa, adjacent to the mouth of the Eau Claire. Police speculate that he was attempting to reach the offices of Dr. Trevelyan Curtis on Barstow Street, where he might force the doctor into treating his wounds prior to making good his escape in the wake of his dastardly deed in the dark alley.

"Whatever Weister's motivation, it came to naught, for faint from loss of blood, he collapsed on the bridge, whereupon a westbound freight passed over him.

"The gruesome results to Weister's person were discovered not long after first light by two sawmill hands, Frederick Bornbach and Albert Sternytzki, who were crossing the bridge en route to their shift at the Daniel Shaw Lumber Company. Weister's head, shoulders, and upper torso had been severed from . . ."

Jeremy's father paused. "Well, we don't have to read those details." He ran a finger down the column. "Here we are:

"Police chief Maurice Cochrane told *Leader* editors that the evidence makes the police reconstruction of events if not incontrovertible at least highly probable, particularly in light of the low reputation associated with both Cripshank and Weister. No further investigation is contemplated."

Mr. Callahan folded the newspaper and tossed it onto the pile that had accumulated in his absence. "Well, there's a bad end to a bad man and a sad end to a sad man. And all over a few trinkets that Fitch would have had me throw away."

Uncle Mac nodded. "The jackal and the lion. I doubt that any will mourn for long. I feel sorry for Cripshank's family, though."

On the far side of the room, Jeremy hugged himself in the shadows.

Neither Lester nor Two-Horse made any sign to him in the days following. Lester polished the fancy harness so that Iris could draw the hearse in the outrageously expensive funeral Hans Weister had ordered in his will. But too many creditors revealed themselves before the appointed day, and the sheriff ordered the undertaker to skip the expense of a funeral no one except the curious and the spiteful would attend anyway.

Life went on. The maiden Crescent Moon received coat after coat of paint until she shone with a deep luster. Watching Two-Horse and Uncle Mac select and occasionally argue over colors, Jeremy felt the terror start to lift from his heart. A bad man had met a bad end, a sad man a sad end—endings for which he could take no blame.

The steam whistle of Valley One gave a last cry, the mournful wail echoing off the shores of the empty river as the great saws whined to a stop. The last log had been milled and the last great drive was history. Soon it would become mythology inhabited by mighty men whose deeds like the vanished forest would become mightier and less believable with every retelling.

Willie came to see Jeremy a final time. They had ice cream sodas together and then stood outside Callahan's, too much separating them to have much to say. Jeremy nudged Willie's carpetbag with his foot. "What are you taking with you?"

"Some clothes, a blanket. Nothing much else to take. Ain't like I'm a reader or anything . . . Uh, I did take my baseball mitt. Took Eddie's, too, in case I run into him down the road somewhere."

"What are you going to do?"

"Get on a threshing crew. Ain't much wheat around here now that the farmers are raising corn and cows, but I hear tell there's wheat for about a thousand miles out on the plains." He smiled. "You wanta come along?"

Jeremy avoided his eyes. "I wouldn't be any good on a threshing crew. They'll put you to work as a man. Me . . ." He shrugged.

Willie nodded. "Well, working in a mill kind of hardens up a guy some." He took a deep breath of the morning air and grinned. "Gosh, I'm glad to be out of there. I've had my fill of mill work. Give me the open air and the sky above. Well, I guess I'd better be getting." He leaned down for his bag.

Jeremy felt a sudden panic. "You didn't tell me how things have been going since . . . Well, you know."

Willie shrugged. "Pa wasn't no account to anybody. Never had been. Ma and the little kids will be all right. Ma's pretty good at making do, and I'll send 'em something once I get work."

"How about Agnes?"

"Agnes lit out two or three weeks ago, and I doubt she'll be back. All she ever cared about was getting out of here.

But she'll find it hard wherever she goes, I expect. That's just the way things are for her."

"But why do you have to leave? There's gonna be work—"

"No, there's not, Jeremy. Not good work. Not for a long time. Now Pa, he was never worth a damn. And I'm sorry to say it, but neither is Agnes. But Eddie is. He's gonna make something of himself. And I'm sure gonna try. But I can't do it here." He compressed his lips and then slapped Jeremy on the shoulder with a hard, strong hand. "You take care, buddy. Get that fancy learning and someday I'll be able to say I knew you when." He grabbed his bag and started away.

For a moment Jeremy's throat was too tight for him to say anything, but then he called, "Tell Eddie hello for me when you see him."

Willie waved over his shoulder.

Uncle Mac used a fine brush to paint Crescent Moon's eyes a fawn brown. He stepped back, and the three of them gazed at her, each reading in the still face something defying exact description: a wisdom of things remembered, of things eternal. There was no hint that if given life she might suddenly speak secrets, only that she might smile with their knowledge.

"So, have you nearly finished?" They turned to see Nancy Two-Horse in the doorway, her arms full of parcels. She set them by the door and came across the room to stand beside Crescent Moon. "Can you tell us apart?"

"The silly one talks too much and is disrespectful to her elders," Two-Horse said. "A foolish girl. The other is a woman."

Nancy turned to Crescent Moon, looking her up and down, seemingly unabashed by her beauty. "Well, you should mind your manners, young lady." She pursed her lips. "I will say that the clothes never looked so good on me." She turned to Uncle Mac, suddenly serious. "She is very beautiful, McAlester."

"Thank you, Nancy. Her beads need another coat or two of paint. And so does the detail on her belt and moccasins. But I'm going to let this coat harden for a few days before we finish."

Uncle Mac sent Jeremy across the street for a pitcher of lemonade. They sat under the maple, talking. "Uncle," Nancy said, "I'm thinking of going home. My cousin Enos Halfaday came to see me. We went to the fair together. He and his wife are starting a new school on the reserve. An Indian school for Indian children. It will be a great experiment. He says I can work there if I like. His wife will even help me finish my teaching certificate."

"How is my nephew? I heard he married that white schoolteacher from New Post."

"Yes, and she is very nice. She was ill with morning sickness on the day of the fair but made Enos and me go without her." She turned to Jeremy. "I waved to you and your father from the Ferris wheel but you didn't see us."

"I'm sorry. I did see you in one of the pavilions. I thought he was . . ." Jeremy hesitated, feeling his face color.

"You thought he was perhaps a boyfriend? A suitor?"

"Uh, I guess. Something like that."

Her smile widened for a moment. "I see." She turned to talk again to Two-Horse about the school.

At long last, Two-Horse nodded. "The government people may fight you, since they think only they know what to teach the Anishinaabe. But I think you will win. I say go, *nindanis*, and teach the children."

"Thank you, Uncle. Mrs. Paquette has been kind to me, so I will stay until she's trained another girl to make hats in my place. And I will see you all before I go. Now I'll have one more look at the river maiden, then my little cousin can help me carry my parcels to the trolley." She smiled at Jeremy.

The next morning Uncle Mac was lettering a sign. Jeremy stood at his shoulder to read it:

McALESTER COMMERCIAL SIGNS
SIGNS FOR THE BUSINESS OR SHOP
EXPERT LETTERING
FREE INSTALLATION
BY APPOINTMENT ONLY

"You're going to paint signs?" Jeremy asked in astonishment.

"Only those I can make here. I'll leave painting on windows to others."

"But what about carving?"

"Oh, I'll do that if anyone wants any done. But that time's passed, I think. And you've got to change with the times."

"I thought you'd close up. You know, retire and go fishing."

Uncle Mac looked at Crescent Moon, standing beautiful in the morning light. "I thought so, too, before I carved her. But recently I've been thinking maybe I'm too young to give up work entirely. I'm still a few years short of seventy, and why not paint a few signs, I'm thinking. But I am going to go fishing more. This is going to be a by-appointment-only business."

"What's Two-Horse think?"

Uncle Mac chuckled. "He's talking of a change, too. Said maybe he'll move to the reservation at last. Maybe even go looking for one more wife before he dies."

"He wouldn't!"

"Why not? There's ginger in the old boy yet. He went home yesterday to look over his garden. Said he had a yen for a trolley ride. Well, let's see how our girl is doing this morning." He went to Crescent Moon and bent to study the paint on her dress.

"We're not going to give her another coat of paint, are we? She's already had half a dozen."

"Seven. No, I think we're done except for the beads on her headdress and belt. I still want to give the rest of the paint another couple of days, though. There are always drips and runs to rub away when you're doing detail work, and I want to make sure the rest of her paint is as hard as it's going to get."

Jeremy looked around the shop, suddenly at a loss for something to do. "Well, maybe I'll go look around. See if I can find a sandlot game."

"Good. Have fun."

Jeremy left the shop bemused by how so many people he knew—Willie, Eddie, Nancy, Agnes, now even Two-Horse and Uncle Mac—could so confidently put endings on huge parts of their lives and almost carelessly start anew. He found a baseball game, played well, and came home tired and happy in the late afternoon to sweep Callahan's. Yet, throughout the day, the sense of standing between beginnings and possibilities gnawed at him.

Chapter 15

☽

After nearly a month of sunny weather, it rained, and the delay in finishing Crescent Moon stretched into a week. Jeremy helped his father around the store. Mr. Callahan sent Mr. Fitch on a few days' vacation, and the old man went grumbling off to visit his sister in Barron. "She's in for a treat," Mr. Callahan commented. Jeremy laughed.

When there was nothing to do in the store, Jeremy read past issues of *Harper's Weekly* and tried again to read *The Old Curiosity Shop*, but found it as boring as ever. He had fallen behind with his piano practice and, with Professor Hauenstein's gentle prodding, tried to catch up. Then finally, when he thought he was about to go mad with boredom, the gray sky lightened and the sun broke through.

On the first sunny day, Nancy came to the shop. "Have you seen Uncle?" she asked.

Uncle Mac frowned. "No. He went home to tend his garden. I thought he probably stayed there until the rain let up, knowing that I wouldn't paint in damp weather."

Nancy stood uncertainly in the doorway. "He told me he'd come to help me return the dress and belt we borrowed.

But he didn't. Now I'm worried. I should go see if he is all right."

Uncle Mac shook his head. "You shouldn't go all that way by yourself, Nancy. Many men are on the roads now that the mills have closed. It would be safer if you had someone with you."

Nancy smiled at Jeremy. "Perhaps my little cousin could be my protector."

Jeremy felt his chest swell. "Could I, Uncle Mac?"

"I don't see any reason why not. But your father's home now, and you should ask him."

Mr. Callahan had no objection, and within an hour Nancy and Jeremy stepped off the trolley at the end of the line. They followed the abandoned railroad tracks past the quarry, which seemed this day not destitute of life but swarming with birds and butterflies, frogs and water bugs.

Nancy moved ahead with a smooth, swinging walk, her long skirt tucked up under her belt so that the tall meadow grass brushed her bare legs. In town she dressed primly like a woman years older. But with her skirt tucked up and her long braids swinging across the back of her bright blouse, she looked more a girl than a woman.

On the bluff above the Chippewa, they sat in the sun to eat the sandwiches Mrs. Higgins had packed. Below them, the wide river flowed lazily through the sunlit morning. Upstream, a crew of lumberjacks, tiny in the distance, crawled along the great catch boom, dismantling the chains and monster tree trunks that had no purpose now that the drives would come no more.

Jeremy glanced often at Nancy, allowing himself to imagine that someday he might be more than a boy to her. He pictured himself as a young man, college degree fresh, stepping into Nancy's schoolhouse, the little Indian children staring in wonder at this strange white man and then giggling when teacher threw her arms about him.

"What are you thinking, little cousin?"

Jeremy looked away quickly. "Nothing."

"You were smiling at nothing?"

He shrugged and looked down to hide his embarrassment. She lifted his chin, her face inches from his, her eyes gentle. "It's all right. I can tell from how you look at me. But a month after I'm gone there will be another girl, perhaps a girl your own age. And after that another and another, until you have forgotten me."

He started to shake his head, to say "Never," but she put a finger to his lips. "It's growing up. White, Indian, it makes no difference. And it's all right." She took her finger away and very gently and very briefly touched her lips to his. "Let's go now."

They rose from the grass. With the feel of Nancy's lips still on his, Jeremy felt an incredible lightness, almost a dizziness. He stared upstream once again, trying to focus his thoughts. The crew of lumberjacks had succeeded in parting the great catch boom, and a boat, its small engine chuffing white puffs, was drawing one end toward shore. And in a moment that he knew he would remember always, Jeremy realized that he, like his country, stood on the threshold of a different time. He felt at once very alone and very free and not the least bit afraid, as he turned to follow Nancy Two-Horse along the bluff above the Chippewa.

Though they knocked and called, Two-Horse did not come to the door. Jeremy took a deep breath and reached for the door handle. Nancy put a hand out to stop him. "No. I must do this."

Jeremy waited by the garden. The corn stood taller than he was, and the pumpkins and squash had begun to turn orange. Weeds grew along untended rows, the forest reaching back to claim the cleared land. Nancy came out of the cabin and stood staring at the garden or perhaps at nothing at all. Finally, she looked at him, tears running down her cheeks. "Uncle has taken the Ghost Road. Go tell McAlester. Ask him to bring a wagon. I will make Uncle ready."

In the dusk, where the path was narrow along the bluff, Lester and Uncle Mac walked on either side of the horses. Nancy rode in the wagon, keening softly beside the body of Two-Horse. Wrapped tightly in a blanket, the old Chippewa seemed very small, his body almost that of a child.

Jeremy and his father followed behind. Jeremy, who hadn't cried at all during the time he'd walked back to town, felt his grief spilling over. "He never got a chance to see Crescent Moon finished," he whispered. "Just a couple more days and . . ." He choked back a sob.

His father put an arm around him. "We have no control over such things, Jeremy. Two-Horse's time came and he had to go whether he wanted to or not. Your mother wanted to live so much to see you grow up. God, how she fought. Fought until there was nothing left of her." His voice grew thick. "That last night, when I doubt that she could hear me anymore, I sat with her. I told her then that it was all right for her to go. That Uncle Mac and I would look after you and raise you in a way that would make her proud." He cleared his throat. "And she would be, too. You will be a man. A fine man."

Jeremy put his head against his father's chest, felt his father's arms encircle him. They stood together that way as the wagon creaked ahead and the river far below flowed on toward the Mississippi and the sea.

Chapter 16

☽

The parlor above Callahan's was too small for a wake, so Mr. Fitch, Arlyn, Jeremy, and his father closed the store and spent the morning pushing shelves and display cases against the walls. Nancy had gone to telegraph her kin and to pack her things, so all day Two-Horse lay alone in the icehouse behind the store.

In the afternoon, with nothing more to do except wait until evening, Jeremy crossed to the shop. Uncle Mac sat before Crescent Moon, a small brush in his big hand, a jar of paint open in front of him. But he was not painting the beads on her belt or in her long black hair. He looked up at Jeremy, his eyes deep with pain. "I cannot seem to begin."

They sat for a long time in silence until finally Uncle Mac put away the brush and the paint. "Let's go get ready. People will start coming soon."

A surprising number of people came to Two-Horse's wake. A few came out of curiosity, others for a drink and a helping from the trays of cold meats, cheeses, breads, and pickles.

Yet most came because Two-Horse had represented something that they tried in their various ways to put into words. No one was quite sure how old he'd been, but he could remember Eau Claire when only a dozen houses clung to the shores of the Chippewa and the forest to the north seemed limitless, "more pine than could be cut in a score of lifetimes."

But in the lifetime of this one man, the forest had been felled and the land cleared for farms; the village had grown into a city; and his tribe—all but those few who chose to live with white people—had fled into the back country of the north. He had witnessed all, and although few could find the proper words to describe their feelings, they knew that in Two-Horse's passing a link in the chain of remembering had parted.

Jeremy's father did not approve of whiskey and served only beer and sarsaparilla at the wake. Still, after a time, the talk grew louder, the recollections more boisterous. Jeremy retreated to his room, where he sat by the window, staring out at the river and the sliver of moon that hung above it.

Uncle Mac knocked softly on the door and stepped into the room. "It's time to finish her. Will you come?"

Jeremy nodded. He pulled back the covers on his bed and positioned the lump of his pillow and his extra blanket.

Uncle Mac laughed softly. "You don't think your father would understand?"

"Do you?"

Uncle Mac shook his head.

They crossed to the shop and drew the shades tight. They brought the lamps close to Crescent Moon and began to paint. There seemed a thousand beads, each one requiring the lightest touch with the point of a brush and no more, lest the paint run.

Jeremy worked from the back, along her belt, while Uncle Mac started on her headdress. They moved bead by bead around her. Jeremy lost track of the hours as the night became a deep drum where time itself seemed to reverberate. At last, and much to his surprise, he found himself where he had begun. He searched for beads he'd missed but found none. "I'm finished."

"Go curl up in the chair. I have a little way to go yet."

Jeremy watched from the chair as he had on the night Uncle Mac had carved Crescent Moon's face. And though he did not look, he had the sense that Two-Horse, or some part of him, squatted yet in the corner, practicing a silence no white man could achieve.

He slept and woke in broad daylight to the sound of the front door being thrown open. His father stormed into the shop. "Oh, for heaven's sake! What are you two—"

Uncle Mac stepped back from Crescent Moon, and the sight of her snuffed Mr. Callahan's tirade. For a long minute he stared. Jeremy came over and stood beside him, equally awestruck. The night had transformed the maiden's beauty a final time, made it at once unearthly and of the earth— like the beauty of the moon riding high in a night sky as it silently moved the tides and the continents.

"I see," Mr. Callahan said. He shook his head as if to clear it. "All right, both of you. Go get washed and changed.

One of Two-Horse's brothers and Nancy's cousin Enos came in on the morning train. In an hour we're taking him to the station. Lester's already getting Iris ready. Now go, I know what to do here."

"The paint—" Uncle Mac started to say.

"Is wet. I'll be careful. Now go. Hurry." He stripped off his coat.

By the time Jeremy had washed, changed, and rushed back down the stairs, his father and Arlyn had maneuvered Crescent Moon through the door of the shop to the street. A small crowd gathered, staring in wonder. "Stand by her," Mr. Callahan said to Jeremy, and crossed to the store.

Jeremy heard the jangle of the silver harness and turned to see the hearse coming up the Sunday morning street. Lester, dressed in his black suit, drew Iris to a halt in front of Callahan's. The undertaker said something to him and then climbed down to go inside. A moment later he came out with Nancy. They held the doors open as Mr. Callahan, Uncle Mac, Arlyn, Mr. Fitch, and Two-Horse's nephew and brother, their heads bare, carried the coffin across the sidewalk to the back of the hearse. Jeremy glanced at Crescent Moon, as if he half expected some expression to cross her painted features.

Mr. Callahan spoke briefly to the undertaker and then led Nancy and the two Chippewa men across the street. Uncle Mac hesitated and then followed. The Chippewa men stopped in front of Crescent Moon and studied her. Enos Halfaday, who wore the same stylish clothing Jeremy had seen him in at the fair, turned to Nancy. "She's splendid.

I see you in her." He looked at the older man, who was walking a slow circle around Crescent Moon. "What say you, Uncle?"

The older Indian did not speak for another minute and then replied in Chippewa. Nancy nodded and looked at Uncle Mac. "He says it is a work of magic. That you and his brother were blessed to see into the heart of things. Now the Anishinaabe will have something for people to remember them by, even if our whole race dies."

Enos grinned. "Which isn't going to happen. Not when we take back our schools and the education of our children."

Uncle Mac shuffled, then extended his hand to Two-Horse's brother. "Yes, I was blessed in many ways."

Mr. Callahan pulled Jeremy into the circle, where there were more handshakes and words of parting and thanks before the undertaker frowned at his watch and signaled that it was time to leave for the station.

Nancy paused a moment by Jeremy. "Good bye, little cousin. You will always be welcome at Lac Courte Oreilles."

"Thank you," Jeremy said, knowing how small the chances were that he would ever see her again.

"Look after McAlester." She turned a final time to Crescent Moon. "And this powerful girl."

"I will," Jeremy said.

And watching her walk away in the morning light, Jeremy felt neither sadness nor longing, but only an astonishing fullness of heart.

Epilogue

☽

Jeremy graduated from Brown University and became an official of the Bureau of Indian Affairs, where he was an advocate of tribal control of schools. He married and was widowed twice, living on rich in children and grandchildren to the brink of another new century. Although he thought of her often, he never saw Nancy Two-Horse again.

Nancy married an Episcopal clergyman of mixed blood in 1919. They had four children whose care did not prevent Nancy from continuing a teaching career that spanned nearly sixty years. She died in 1978.

Uncle Mac lived another fifteen years after finishing Crescent Moon, painting signs and occasionally carving until a week before he died peacefully in his sleep in 1927.

Mike Callahan eventually remarried and, with his wife's encouragement, turned from business to politics. He served eight terms in the state legislature, where he earned a reputation as a champion of workers' rights. He returned to Eau Claire to hold a variety of civic posts. He died full of plans and accomplishments in 1953.

Murphy recovered enough of his eyesight to do odd jobs around the farm until a sudden heart attack carried him off a month short of his fortieth birthday in 1917.

Soupy lived to be nearly a hundred, never wasting a word or the opportunity to do a kindness.

When the livery stable closed on the eve of America's entry into World War I, Lester moved to Detroit. In an irony he always appreciated, he spent the rest of his working life assembling automobiles. He married a widow with five children, greatly enjoying family life after his long bachelorhood. He died in 1946.

Agnes Cripshank died in 1918 in the worldwide influenza epidemic that would eventually kill twenty-two million people.

In 1926, fourteen years after he left Eau Claire, Willie Cripshank joined a line of men applying for a job as a mechanic at a farm implement dealership in Sidney, Nebraska. The man in line ahead of him was his brother Eddie. They told the dealer that they would give him the work of two for the price of one and a half. No fool, the dealer hired them. Five years later he sold them the business. Cripshank Farm Implement survived the Depression and prospered, supporting two large families of hardworking, sober, and altogether joyous Cripshanks.

Crescent Moon stood in a place of honor in Callahan's for a dozen years. When the store burned in 1924, Arlyn and an ailing, unsentimental Mr. Fitch wrestled her out the door a step ahead of the flames. By the time the store was rebuilt a year later, she had become a permanent fixture beside the high bench in the circuit court. She remained there until she was somehow misplaced or stolen during the remodeling of the courthouse in the 1950s. Her current whereabouts are unknown.

The great white pine forest was gone forever. Northern Wisconsin proved poor farming country and much of the abandoned cutover grew back in maple, birch, and aspen. Starting with the Civilian Conservation Corps in the 1930s, government and commercial interests began reforesting the land, depending heavily on the hearty Norway pine. The work continues.

Bearing the waters of the Manitowish, Couderay, Jump, Thornapple, Brunet, Flambeau, Eau Claire, Red Cedar, and a hundred smaller rivers and streams, the mighty Chippewa still flows southwest toward the Mississippi and the sea.